DOCTOR WHO
WARRIORS OF THE DEEP

DOCTOR WHO
WARRIORS OF THE DEEP

Based on the BBC television serial by Johnny Byrne by
arrangement with the British Broadcasting Corporation

TERRANCE DICKS

A TARGET BOOK

published by
the Paperback Division of
W. H. ALLEN & Co. PLC

A Target Book
Published in 1984
By the Paperback division of
W.H. Allen & Co. PLC
44 Hill Street, London, W1X 8LB

First published in Great Britain by
W. H. Allen & Co. PLC 1984

The BBC producer of *Warriors of the Deep* was
John Nathan-Turner, the director was Pennant Roberts

Printed and bound in Great Britain by
Hunt Barnard Printing Ltd., Aylesbury, Bucks.

ISBN 0 426 19561 2

Contents

1

The Intruder

The Base might have been in space.

It had been built at enormous effort and expense. It was surrounded by a hostile environment – into which humans could venture only with elaborate life-support systems.

The Base was the nucleus of an elaborate attack and defence system. Its inhabitants lived lives of constant tension, perpetually under the shadow of planetary annihilation.

It might have been in space – but it wasn't.

Space stations had proved too vulnerable, too exposed to spy-satellites and the searing blast of laser-beams. In the early years of the twenty-first century, mankind concealed many of its weapons of destruction beneath the seas.

Sea Base Four crouched like a giant metal spider in the black depths of the ocean floor. It waited, like every other Sea Base, for any hint of an attack from the other side. Such an attack would unleash a swarm of proton missiles in massive retaliation.

East confronted West, hostile, suspicious, waiting.

Yet neither side realised that there were other enemies beneath the sea – beings equally hostile to both sides alike, creatures who regarded *all* mankind as primitive apes who had stolen the planet Earth from its rightful owners. Mankind's oldest enemies had awakened once more – and they were poised to attack.

Outside Sea Base Four was only the cold green darkness of the ocean depths. Inside, everything was gleaming, modern, brightly lit. The predominating colour was a dazzling white, as if designed to counter the threatening blackness that lurked outside.

Sea Base personnel moved busily along the corridors and catwalks, wearing the distinctive cross-belted coveralls of the Undersea Service. Uniforms were colour-coded according to rank and function – blue for officers, reds and greens and greys for the different specialisations. Moving amongst the brighter colours were the drab khaki uniforms of the Radiation Squad, responsible for the Base's nuclear reactor. They alone wore side-arms and helmets – in the unlikely event of the Base being attacked, they would double as marine guards.

In the central control room, referred to as the Bridge, instrument consoles hummed gently, glowing blips chased each other across monitor screens, and the steady electronic beep of scanner systems filled the air. Commander Vorshak sat at the central command console, staring broodingly at a monitor screen. Vorshak was a tall, dark-haired man in his mid-forties. Elegant in his dark-blue coverall, Vorshak had the rugged good looks of a recruiting-poster hero, much to his own embarrassment.

Clustered around him were his officers: the ever-calm, coldly reserved Controller Nilson; Lieutenant Preston, a pleasant capable looking woman in her twenties; Lieutenant Bulic, the burly combat officer in charge of the marine guard.

There was an emergency.

Vorshak studied the moving blip on the screen, listened to the steady accompanying electronic beep.

He looked up at Bulic. 'What do *you* think?'

Bulic paused for a moment, assessing the data. 'Too small to be a hunter-killer missile.'

'Could be one of their probes, though, trying to locate our position.'

Vorshak swung round to a nearby sub-console. 'Maddox, let's have a computer scan.'

The computer console stood a little apart from the rest. Beside the console, and linked to it, stood an empty chair with a helmet-like apparatus suspended above – the synch op chair. Somehow people avoided mentioning, or even looking at it. At the console by the chair, Maddox, a thin-faced and nervous young man, sat staring abstractedly in front of him. Vorshak's sudden command jolted him into awareness. Feverishly he set to work, fingers clumsy on the instrument panel.

Vorshak watched him impatiently. Maddox was new, a temporary emergency replacement, and Vorshak had little patience with him.

From a nearby console a dark-haired young woman with attractive oriental features looked sympathetically at Maddox's fumblings. Lieutenant Karina was the Scanner Officer, and she had been worried about Maddox for some time. The boy was close to breaking point, and Vorshak was pushing him too hard. It could be a bad mistake. Unobtrusively she moved to help him.

The undersea vessel that was causing so much concern on Sea Base Four was long, slender and cigar-shaped, and it was travelling away from the Base at incredible speed.

Its greenish hull had a rough, irregular surface, like something grown rather than manufactured.

The vessel sped to the centre of a low range of undersea volcanic mountains. For a moment it hovered over one of the larger craters, then sank down slowly out of sight.

The interior of the vessel too had a strangely organic look. Certainly there was a control room, with instruments roughly equivalent to those on a human ship. Yet, like the craft itself, these oddly shaped instruments seemed grown rather than built, and the atmosphere here was one of dark and shadowy gloom, shot with greenish light.

The ship was not human in origin, and neither were those who inhabited it. The immensely tall, robed figures were brown-skinned with great crested heads and huge bulging eyes. Their slow, almost stately movements, their coldly measured speech-tones gave evidence of their reptilian origin. They were Silurians.

The eldest and the most high-ranking was Icthar; he was the sole survivor of the Silurian Triad, the warrior-scientist élite that had ruled Earth in the days before man. His two companions were Scibus and Tarpok.

Scibus looked up from an instrument console and spoke with the calm dignity that Silurians gave every pronouncement. 'No hostile movement is registered. There is no pursuit.'

'Excellent,' said Icthar, in the same deep, impressive tones.

Tarpok said, 'Is it wise to risk provoking them, Icthar?'

The great crested head swung round towards him. 'We shall continue to monitor the activities of the humans, Tarpok. But we shall also take care to remain undetected until we are ready to strike.'

'We've lost it, Commander,' reported Lieutenant Karina matter-of-factly. 'The trace got fainter and fainter – then suddenly it cut out.'

Vorshak looked across at Maddox. 'Computer analysis?'

'Seems to be – *organic* in structure. There was some heat radiation . . .'

'Could it have been volcanic debris?'

Controller Nilson said, 'It's more than possible, Commander. We're close to the oceanic fault here.'

Vorshak touched a switch and the monitor screen punched up a view of the exterior of the Base. The sea-bed stretched into the distance, its monotony broken by occasional volcanic rock formations. Vorshak knew that Sea Base sensors were almost *too* efficient. Warning signals could be triggered by a particularly dense shoal of fish, an outsize shark – or by the missile that might one day blow them all to eternity. Vorshak wanted desperately to accept the reassuring explanation, and this very fact made him somehow suspicious of it. The trace *could* have been a fish, or volcanic debris – or it could have been something else.

This was a particularly dangerous time in Earth's long and stormy history. A period of maximum tension, between two colossal powers. The different warring groups and countries and philosophies had solidified into two massive groupings, East Bloc and West Bloc. There was no communication, no trust between them. Each poured out a steady stream of propaganda, blackening the other side. Worst of all, each side had come to believe in its own propaganda, to believe that the opposing Bloc was populated not by human beings much like themselves but by cold-hearted ruthless monsters.

Armed satellites filled the skies, each side observing

the other with constant suspicion. There were human spies too – espionage and sabotage flourished as never before. Each side had one overriding fear, that the other would come up with some advantage, some new weapon, that would make its aggressive use worthwhile.

Strangely enough, the invention of the proton missile had made matters worse. In the days of the atomic stalemate there had at least been the hope that no one would be fool enough to start a war that could only end in an uninhabitable planet. Now that check was removed. The proton missiles destroyed life, not property, and they were radiation-free. Now perhaps it might be possible to win a global war – *if* you struck first, and struck hard enough. Dividing the Earth between them, East Bloc and West Bloc scrutinised each other with paranoid fear.

Suppose some new weapon *had* been invented, thought Vorshak. Some super-missile, some invincible submarine with the power to knock out the Sea Bases. Perhaps the East Bloc *was* preparing to strike first . . .

Vorshak became aware that his fears were running away with him. He would watch and wait, he decided. And at the first sign of hostile action, he would strike.

The Doctor looked complacently round the newly refurbished TARDIS control room. The time rotor was rising and falling smoothly, the instruments showed them to be on course. Could it be that for once something was going right?

The Doctor, in his fifth incarnation, was a slender, fair-haired young man with a pleasant, open face. He was dressed, somewhat incongruously, in the costume of an Edwardian cricketer – striped trousers, fawn frock-coat wth red piping, white sweater and open-necked shirt.

He looked up as another, much younger man came in. Turlough, one of the Doctor's current companions, wore the dark blazer and flannels, and straggly striped tie of the perpetual public schoolboy. There was something a little off-key about Turlough, a hint of the shifty and unreliable. Thin-faced and red-haired, he looked as if he might be the school bully – or the school sneak.

He nodded towards the console. 'How are we doing?'

'On target, it seems.' Without looking up the Doctor went on casually, 'Why did you change your mind – about going home?'

'I thought I would learn more if I stayed with you.'

The Doctor looked up, raising an eyebrow. There was something ambiguous about the answer he thought, just as there was about Turlough himself.

'It's true,' said Turlough defensively.

'Of course.'

'I mean it!'

Perhaps he did, thought the Doctor. You never knew with Turlough. 'All right, I believe you. But I'm a bit doubtful about how resolute you'll remain.'

'Time will tell.'

'Yes, indeed,' said the Doctor thoughtfully. 'Aboard the TARDIS it always does.'

The console buzzed and the Doctor flipped a switch.

'Where are we going?'

'Earth.'

'What for?'

'I promised to show Tegan a little of her planet's future.'

There was another beep. 'Almost there. Could you go and find Tegan, let her know?'

Commander Vorshak looked on as Bulic made a quick check of all the Sea Base warning systems. 'Nothing?'

13

'Nothing,' grunted Bulic. He scowled at the monitor screen.

'What's bothering you then?'

'I think we should launch a reconnaissance probe.'

'Forever cautious, Bulic!'

'I've served too long in Sea Bases not to be. Given how unstable the current political situation is . . . well, an unexpected attack would not be – unexpected.'

'Very well, Bulic, have it your way. We'll launch an unmanned probe.'

Somewhere in the side of the Base, a hatch slid open and a slender swordfish-like missile sped away into the blackness of the sea.

It would patrol the area around the base in a random pattern, collecting and transmitting data and bringing it back for evaluation – if it returned, that is.

Vorshak grinned ironically at his subordinate. 'Happy, Bulic?'

'Yes sir. Thank you, sir.'

Vorshak glanced across at Maddox. 'Better stay alert. If there *is* activity outside the Base we could go to missile run. So stand by.'

'Yes, sir,' said Maddox.

Vorshak glanced curiously at him, wondering if the boy was ill. He was pale and shivering, like someone fighting off a fever.

Suddenly Maddox jumped to his feet, and almost ran from the Bridge.

Maddox took refuge in the main computer bay, a peaceful area just off the main control room, where row upon row of computer banks hummed peacefully to themselves.

Maddox had never wanted to be a synch op.

Unfortunately for him, he was one of the few people with the ability to mesh his mind with a computer. Once his talent had been discovered in one of the regular Government tests, he had little choice but to volunteer.

The position was well paid, it carried a great deal of prestige, but the strain and responsibility were enormous. All through his training, Maddox had dreaded the time when the full responsibility of a missile run would fall upon his shoulders – a run that might be just another simulation or might, equally well, be the real thing. His training assignment to Sea Base Four had only increased his fears.

At first it hadn't been too bad. People had been unexpectedly kind and helpful, Lieutenant Karina in particular.

Originally Maddox's job had been to trail Michaels, the Base's regular synch op, standing always at his elbow, watching everything he did, taking over only when nothing of any real importance was going on.

Then there had been Michaels' sudden, shockingly unexpected death. Maddox had been thrust into the hot seat – and there he must stay until a fully trained synch op arrived to replace him.

Somehow Maddox had managed to get by – until now. But the crisis had brought back all his fears with redoubled strength. He couldn't go on any longer. He couldn't . . . He slumped helplessly against the wall, his head pressed against the smooth metal of an olive-green computer cabinet. He was shivering with fear.

In the Silurian ship, Icthar was studying an instrument console. Scibus approached. 'The Sea Base has launched a probe.'

'The Myrka will deal with it.'

Tarpok was working on an instrument bank on another part of the control area. 'We are ready to begin, Icthar.'

'Good.' Icthar bowed his head. 'This is a solemn moment. For thousands of years our Sea Devil brothers have lain entombed, waiting patiently for this day. Come.'

Icthar led the way down a steeply sloping passage to the door of a giant chamber in the lower part of the ship. The door was transparent, though at the moment it was obscured by a thick coating of ice.

'It concerns me that our brothers may not awaken as we have planned,' said Tarpok gloomily. 'Their long period of hibernation may have caused muscular and organic deterioration.'

Icthar said philosphically, 'We shall soon know. Proceed, Tarpok!'

Tarpok placed a clawed hand on the control nodule set close to the chamber entrance. For a time nothing happened. Then slowly, very slowly, the ice began to melt, and they could look through the transparent door.

It gave onto a huge chamber, an undersea cavern. Icy mists drifted about the floor. The chamber was filled with row upon row of tall, shrouded shapes.

'Proceed with the process of revival,' ordered Icthar.

Maddox raised his head as Karina came into the computer bay.

She looked at him in concern. 'What's the matter? What are you doing here?'

'I can't do it! I can't go on.'

'Of course you can!'

'You saw me out there. I was shaking . . . I'm not fit.'

'You'd never have been sent to the Sea Base if there was any doubt about your fitness for the job.'

16

'Look, I'm a student on attachment,' said Maddox desperately. 'I was sent to the Sea Base to study an experienced synch operator in action – not to take his place. I'm just not ready.'

'You've got to be. Until Michaels' replacement arrives. There just isn't anyone else.'

'I'm well aware of that! I'd feel a lot happier if there'd been a proper investigation into Lieutenant Michaels' death.'

'Michaels was careless – there was an accident. There's nothing to investigate.'

'I worked with Michaels long enough to get to know him. He was careful to the point of paranoia, obsessively careful. A man like that doesn't electrocute himself carrying out simple maintenance.'

'Have you reported your suspicions to Commander Vorshak?'

'Of course. But he's just not interested. He just keeps on telling me that this is a marvellous opportunity for me to gain what he calls "hard experience".'

'He's right.'

'Maybe he is. But if we do go to missile alert, I just won't be able to cope.'

'Listen to me,' said Karina urgently. 'Maybe you're not quite ready to be a fully-fledged synch operator yet, but don't throw your entire career away now. Lieutenant Michaels' replacement arrives the day after tomorrow. Just sit things out – there may not even be a missile run before then anyway.'

'I suppose you're right. I'll try . . .'

She patted him on the shoulder. 'That's the idea. Now, come on back to the Bridge . . .'

The time rotor was motionless. The Doctor was casting a thoughtful eye on the centre console.

Turlough stood watching the Doctor with an air of deep suspicion.

Next to Turlough, looking equally suspicious, was an attractive girl with dark hair. Her rainbow-coloured dress was a vivid splash of colour in the control room. This was Tegan, the Doctor's other companion. She was an Australian air-hostess, whose involvement with the Doctor had taken her on journeys far beyond the routes of any airline.

'Now what?' demanded Turlough. 'What's gone wrong now?'

'Oh, nothing really! It's my own fault. I should have changed the relativity unit before we set off.'

'We *are* where we should be, though?' asked Tegan. The Doctor didn't reply, and Tegan's voice hardened. 'Aren't we?'

'Oh yes – well, more or less. We're very close to Earth. In orbit just above the atmosphere belt.'

'So what's the problem?'

'Oh, just a slight hiccup with our time-zones. We're a bit too advanced. Sorry.'

Tegan gave him a withering glance, and turned away.

Turlough had just switched on the scanner screen. 'Doctor, look!'

The screen was occupied by a sinister robotic shape, a space satellite bristling with weapons.

'What is it?' whispered Tegan.

'A robot weapons system. It seems to be examining us.'

A booming metallic voice spoke over the intercom. 'This is Sentinel Six. You have entered a forbidden military zone. Transmit your security clearance code immediately.'

The Doctor shot a quick urgent glance at Turlough. 'Re-set the cell cut-out,' he whispered. Raising his

18

voice he said, 'Calling Sentinel Six. Could you repeat your instructions please?'

The metallic voice spoke again with the same mechanical calm. 'You have entered a forbidden military zone. Transmit your security clearance immediately. Repeat: transmit your security clearance, or you will be destroyed.'

2

The Traitors

While Turlough worked frantically at the console behind him, the Doctor raised his voice. 'Sentinel Six! We have no hostile intentions. Our presence here is purely temporary. All we need is a brief time to alter our co-ordinates.'

There was no response.

'Now what?' demanded Tegan. 'What's it *doing*?'

The Doctor hurried to join Turlough at the console. 'Thinking things over!'

Inside the psycho-surgical unit of Sea Base Four, all was calm and peaceful. The brightly lit white-walled room was dominated by the central treatment console, with its attached surgical couch. This was a complex device, not unlike a technologically advanced dentists's chair. In it the patient's body could be held anaesthetised, his bodily functions monitored, whilst the incredibly delicate operations of psycho-surgery were carried out.

A handsome middle-aged woman in the white coveralls of the Medical Section was busy checking over this complex piece of apparatus. Her name was Solow, and she was Sea Base Four's Psycho-Surgeon.

Controller Nilson, Sea Base Four's second-in-command, came quietly into the room.

'It is time to move, Doctor Solow. We have found our man.'

'Maddox?'

'Yes. You were right about him. He is temperamentally unsuited for his work – which gives us our opportunity.'

'I am pleased to hear it. I must admit I was a little concerned. I feared I might have made an inaccurate diagnosis.'

'You can stop worrying – indeed you can congratulate yourself. The unfortunate accident to Lieutenant Michaels has paid off, despite all your scruples.'

Doctor Solow's face was strained. Like Nilson, she was an ideological convert to the cause of the East Bloc. In fact, it was Nilson himself who had converted and recruited her. She was at heart a kind and even generous woman, genuinely distressed at the suffering and injustice in the world around her. Disappointed in her career, left alone by the death of her husband and her parents, she had fallen an easy prey to Nilson's arguments. He had persuaded her that the East Bloc philosophy of uniformity, obedience and central control was the answer to all life's problems. Once the East Bloc ruled supreme, suffering and injustice would vanish magically from the world. Of course, in order to achieve this great victory certain sacrifices would have to be made. Occasionally ruthless and unpleasant methods must be used.

During her association with Nilson, Doctor Solow had fallen completely under his spell. Like him, she had come to accept that most terrible of creeds, that the end justifies the means. However, unlike Nilson she did not find it easy to suppress all conscience in the cause of political expediency.

'You are a hard man, Nilson. I'm a doctor,

21

remember. Murder doesn't come easily to someone of my training.'

'Stop bleating!' Like many political converts Nilson had become a complete fanatic, if anything more ruthless than the masters he served. 'We have been waiting a very long time for an opportunity such as this.'

'I realise that, but – '

'Nothing must go wrong. If your conscience bothers you, Doctor Solow, lock it away in a box until our task is completed!'

Weapons were trained on the TARDIS, the sinister shape of Sentinel Six filled the scanner screen.

'Hurry, Doctor,' pleaded Tegan. 'That thing isn't going to hang there contemplating its navel for ever.'

The Doctor was working at frantic speed. 'Don't panic, Tegan, I'm doing my best.'

In theory, the TARDIS was invulnerable, but there had been weaknesses in its defence systems of late. Even if they survived the first blast of Sentinel Six's weaponry, they couldn't just sit there, attracting the hostile attention of the entire planet.

The voice of Sentinel Six interrupted the Doctor's thoughts. 'This is Sentinel Six. You have been classified as a hostile intruder.'

Without looking up from the console the Doctor shouted, 'Listen to me, Sentinel Six. We are *not* hostile and we are unarmed.'

'Repeat: transmit your security clearance codes or you will be destroyed. This is your final warning.'

'Just give us a little more time and we'll be on our way.'

'Doctor, look!' screamed Tegan.

A massive energy-ball was speeding from Sentinel Six towards the TARDIS. It struck, and the TARDIS jolted and spun. Sentinel Six vanished from the screen, and a high energy-whine filled the control room. 'We're falling,' called the Doctor. 'We're out of control!'

Never at his best in times of personal danger, Turlough went pale. 'We're going to crash!'

'Not if I can perform a quick materialisation flip-flop,' said the Doctor calmly. His hands flickered over the controls, and the time rotor shuddered into life, rose and fell rapidly for a moment, and then cut out. The Doctor opened a flap on the console and peered hopefully inside. 'Well, that's stage one!'

'Commander!' called Bulic.

Vorshak hurried over to the defence console. 'What is it?'

'The reconnaissance probe has stopped transmitting data, sir. It just stopped.'

'A breakdown?'

'Either that or it's been destroyed.'

Vorshak raised his voice in command. 'Perimeter defence, stand by! Lieutenant Karina, feed the co-ordinates of any hostile vessel directly to the defence system. We'll blast it out of the water.'

'I can't, sir,' said Karina helplessly. 'The only thing registering on the scanners is some form of marine life.'

Lieutenant Preston looked puzzled. 'That's impossible. There's nothing out there strong enough to destroy a reconnaissance probe.'

Bulic crossed to study Karina's console. 'Karina's right. There's nothing out there but organic life.'

Suddenly an alarm siren sounded. Everyone turned to look at the main monitor screen. The message they all dreaded was flashing on the screen: 'MISSILE RUN', and beneath it in smaller letters: 'Green Alert'.

Maddox was staring at the words in fascinated horror.

'Maddox!' snapped Vorshak. 'Don't just sit there – verify.'

Maddox operated computer controls with trembling fingers. He studied the data on his read-out screen. 'The computer has started countdown, sir.'

Vorshak swung round in his chair. 'Assessment, Bulic?'

'Hard to tell, sir. Could be a random practice run, initiated by the computer. Equally well, it could have been triggered off by the intruder sighting and the loss of the probe.'

'Then we must assume the missile run is for real.' Vorshak raised his voice. 'All teams to battle stations.'

Lieutenant Preston spoke into her intercom. 'Battle teams one, two and three, take up defence positions.'

Karina was studying a stream of new data on her read-out screen. 'A report from Sentinel Six in planetary orbit, sir. Sentinel Six has just engaged an unidentified flying object. Attempts to shoot it down were unsuccessful, and it has now disappeared.'

Her announcement only added to the tense atmosphere on the bridge.

Vorshak and his officers sat grimly at their consoles, monitoring the flood of information on the display screens in front of them.

'Missile computer on automatic targeting,' reported Bulic. 'Arming of photon missiles now in progress.'

Suddenly the synch op area came to life. Light beamed down on the chair, which began humming with power.

'Prepare for synch-up,' said Vorshak.

Maddox didn't move.

'Maddox! Take up your position.' Vorshak looked at the trembling figure crouched over the computer console. 'What's wrong, Maddox?'

24

'I can't do it, sir.'

'You must. Without you, our missiles are useless.'

'Do you think I don't realise that?'

'Synch up, Maddox,' ordered Vorshak harshly. 'We need you to find out what the computer is doing. Come on, we could be at war!'

Reluctantly Maddox rose and crossed to the synch chair, and settled himself in place.

Eyes closed he leaned back against the head-rest. Nilson peeled back two tiny patches of hair from Maddox's skull, revealing the electrodes beneath.

'Just relax,' said Nilson gently. 'Assess what the computer tells you, and relay the information to the Commander. Leave the final decision to him.'

'I still have to pull the firing-lever,' muttered Maddox.

'It may not come to that. Now, are you ready?'

Maddox nodded. Nilson touched a control, and the gleaming metal helmet descended over Maddox's head.

Vorshak looked on, concerned. The synch op system had been in operation for a relatively short time. Vorshak had never been happy about it.

So sophisticated was the latest generation of computers that it was literally impossible to deal directly with the speed and complexity of the data they provided. An interpreter was needed, a link between man and machine. That link could only be a human brain, still the finest computer of all – but not every brain was suitable. Synch ops were carefully selected, rigorously trained. Electrodes were surgically implanted in their brains, enabling them to be literally plugged in to the computer complex – synched up – so that they could monitor and interpret the computer's data, giving the Commander the information he needed.

Vorshak knew that the final responsibility was his,

but Maddox was his link to the computer. And if that link did not hold . . .

Maddox shuddered in the chair, and then relaxed.

Nilson said quietly, 'We have synch-up to missile computer, Commander.'

'Go ahead, Maddox.'

Maddox's hands – they were the computer's hands now – began moving swiftly over the keyboard in front of him. 'Missiles locked onto targets, sir.'

A complex pattern of missile tracks appeared on the defence screen. Above it flashed the message – 'MISSILE RUN. RED ALERT'. Collectively, the Bridge held its breath.

The Doctor straightened up from the console. 'We made it!'

'I don't believe it,' said Tegan.

Turlough was equally sceptical. 'I don't think the Doctor does either!'

'Well, it was a little close,' admitted the Doctor. 'Now then, let's see where we are . . .'

'Well, where *are* we?' asked Tegan.

'Still in the same time-zone, at least,' said the Doctor thoughtfully.

'And on Earth?'

'I think so.' The Doctor switched on the scanner, and studied the picture thoughtfully.

It didn't tell him very much. They were in a large open space inside some kind of structure. In the distance a spiral staircase led up to a higher level.

'Well, let's find out,' said the Doctor.

Tegan shivered. 'It's a bit chilly in here.'

Turlough looked around: white-painted metal walls, walkways and staircases and a strange distant sound – could it be the lapping of water? 'We seem to be on some kind of ship.'

The Doctor spotted a circular porthole and went to peer out of it. He could see only murky blackness. 'Or a submarine. There's no movement. We could be on the sea-bed.' He nodded towards the spiral staircase. 'Come on, let's take a look around.'

They began climbing the staircase. None of them noticed that the TARDIS door wasn't properly closed.

Maddox said hoarsely. 'Missiles armed.'

'Prepare firing sequence,' ordered Vorshak.

Maddox's hands moved rapidly over the controls and then became still. His right hand rested on the firing lever. The words 'COUNTDOWN TO IGNITION' flashed up on the screen. On the console before Bulic, a digital clock began its countdown: 60,59,58 . . .

'Countdown to missile launch under way!' announced Bulic.

In total silence, the officers of Sea Base Four waited for the moment that could mean the outbreak of war.

Bulic said harshly, 'Thirty seconds to launch . . .'

Vorshak looked at the diminishing numbers on the screen: 28,27,26. He looked at Maddox, who sat trembling at the console.

Vorshak would give the order, but Maddox must pull the lever. Would he, *could* he do it?

Suddenly an electronic wailing filled the Bridge area, and a new message flashed on the screen. 'SIMULATED MISSILE RUN. ALL CLEAR'.

Vorshak let out a long sigh of relief. 'Well, we can breathe again.'

Maddox flopped forwards on to his console, like a puppet whose taut strings have suddenly been cut.

Vorshak looked at the slumped figure. 'Get him out of here!'

Two guards ran forward and began lifting Maddox from the chair.

'Take him to the PS unit,' said Nilson quickly. 'Doctor Solow will attend to him.'

Vorshak rubbed a hand across his eyes. 'What a time for a practice run!'

Bulic said, 'Commander, you realise the Base is defenceless while Maddox is out of action?'

Preston came to join them. 'And we still have to establish what destroyed our probe – and what Sentinel Six shot at.'

Vorshak nodded wearily. 'Sound the all-clear. But the Base will remain on full alert.'

A strange electronic wailing filled the air.

Tegan looked up. 'What's that noise?'

They were walking along a white-walled metal corridor. The Doctor stopped, studying some lettering on one of the metal sections that made up the wall. It was misted over with condensation. The Doctor rubbed at it with his hand. Turlough passed him a handkerchief.

'Ah, thank you Turlough.' The Doctor rubbed away the condensation. 'Sea Base Four. Ah, yes, a Sea Base, I thought as much!' He handed the handkerchief back to Turlough. 'Thank you.'

'Not at all, Doctor. And the noise?'

'Sounded like an all-clear.'

The noise cut out.

'What *is* this place, Doctor? Some kind of research station?'

'I don't think so, Turlough. I think it's a rather special kind of undersea military colony.'

The end of the corridor was blocked by a sliding door. The Doctor heaved at it, but it wouldn't budge. 'Help me get this door open, Turlough, would you? Yes, an undersea colony. Armed with the sort of missiles that destroy life but leave everything else intact.'

Turlough joined him in heaving at the door. 'Photon missiles, you mean.'

'Very probably . . .'

The door wouldn't budge. The Doctor and Turlough looked helplessly at one another . . .

Tegan slipped in between them, pushed in the other direction left to right, rather than right to left – and the door slid smoothly open. Tegan stepped through, and the Doctor and Turlough followed.

With the endless patience of his reptilian race, Icthar stood waiting by the ice chamber. Through the transparent door he could see clouds of mist rising about the shrouded forms. As yet there was no movement, no sign of life.

Scibus appeared. 'The Sea Base has completed a missile run. It appears that it was merely a practice.'

Icthar inclined his head. 'Then our presence remains undetected. Continue to monitor the activity of the Base. The reactivation process should now be near completion.' He turned to Tarpok. 'Have we any indications of conditions within the chamber?'

'No. The temperature level within is still below the range of our sensors.'

Patiently, Icthar continued his long vigil.

On the bridge, Vorshak like a good commander, was listening to the worries of his subordinates. Finally, he raised a hand, cutting short the discussion. 'We'll remain on full alert . . . and we'll launch another probe. For the moment, that's all we can do.'

Bulic nodded, accepting the decision. 'Very good, sir.' He went off to supervise the launch.

The console beeped. Vorshak leaned forward. 'Bridge.'

Nilson's voice came from the intercom. 'Nilson here

Commander, in the psycho-surgery section. We have a problem with Maddox. I think you should come down.'

'Very well.' Vorshak rose and stretched, cramped after long hours in the command chair. 'Bulic, you're in command, I'll be down in the Psycho-Surgical unit.'

The Doctor and his companions had reached a storage area, filled with an assortment of drums and pressurised cylinders. Racks on the walls held pumps and nozzles and plastic hose, presumably for dispensing the various chemicals.

Tegan looked round. A store room was a store room, she thought. So far her trip into Earth's future wasn't proving very exciting. 'Doctor, what year are we in?'

'Oh, about 2084.'

'Things don't seem to have improved much since my time.'

The Doctor was wandering around, examining the drums. 'I'm afraid they haven't, Tegan. There are now just two power blocs, fingers poised to annihilate each other.' He peered at the markings on one of the drums. 'Good grief! Hexachromite.'

Turlough frowned. 'What do they use that for?'

'It's one of the ingredients of a sealing compound for undersea structures. Harmless to humans, but in its pure state it's lethal to marine life. I thought they'd have banned it by now.'

'Progress doesn't seem to have improved things much,' said Tegan. She led the way out of the store room.

Vorshak, Nilson and Doctor Solow stood looking down at Maddox. He was stretched unconscious on

30

the operating couch.

Vorshak said irritably, 'Well, what's the matter with him?'

Doctor Solow's voice was grave. 'He's suffering from severe stress. I'm sorry, Commander, but it's my considered opinion that he's unfit for duty.'

Vorshak glared angrily at her. 'Unfit? He's got to be fit. I need him. Without a synch operator this Base ceases to have any military function. We're unarmed and defenceless – completely helpless!'

Nilson too looked grave, but inside he was thinking exultantly, 'Precisely, Commander. Helpless. Just as I planned!'

3

Hunted

There was a moment of silence. Both Nilson and Doctor Solow knew that what Vorshak said was literally true. It was on this fact that their scheme depended.

Without a synch op, the Base's missile system could not function. The inclusion of a human brain in the computer-command link-up gave the Western Bloc a vital advantage in the speed of decision-making. It was also the system's weakest link.

Synch op technicians were in short supply. The training was difficult, sometimes dangerous, and only certain specially selected minds could cope. Sometimes, as in the case of Maddox, mistakes were made.

Nilson said, 'I realise Maddox's importance, Commander. You still have one option remaining – though I almost hesitate to mention it.'

'And that is?'

'You could release the duplicate programme disc. Then Doctor Solow could probe deeper into Maddox's mind, break through the barriers and reassure him.'

Vorshak frowned. Synch-op programming was a closely guarded military secret. As far as was known, the Eastern Bloc had not yet achieved it, though they were certainly working on the problem. 'I can't do that. Not without authority from HQ – and I can't ask for authority because we're forbidden to break radio silence while the emergency lasts.'

'If we're to maintain operational efficiency, Commander, it's the only way.'

Vorshak hesitated. To release the duplicate programme disc without proper authority could endanger his career – but to leave the entire base unarmed and helpless would endanger hundreds of lives.

Doctor Solow said gently, 'I'll take full responsibility, sir. There are humanitarian as well as military considerations involved. Unless Maddox is reprogrammed, he'll have a total mental collapse.'

Her intervention tipped the balance. Vorshak crossed to a wall-safe, took an entry-coder from his pocket and punched out a complicated access code. The safe-door slid open. Vorshak removed a gleaming metallic disc and handed it to Nilson.

'Don't let it out of your sight. If it gets into enemy hands –'

'I'll return it as soon as the re-programming is finished,' promised Nilson.

Vorshak nodded and left the PS unit – unaware that the precious disc was in enemy hands already.

Nilson studied the disc exultantly. It represented a valuable espionage coup in itself, though for the moment there was no way to get the information it contained off the Base. More important, it would give Doctor Solow and Nilson total command over the mind of Maddox – and enable them to proceed to the next stage of their plan. Carefully Nilson inserted the disc into the psycho-surgical console.

Doctor Solow was already moving aside the little flaps of artificial skin and hair that covered the synch terminals in Maddox's head. She plugged in the two leads that ran from the console and stood back. Nilson touched the control and the programme began to run.

Maddox stirred and moaned, then relaxed. Nilson studied him uneasily. 'You're sure this will work?'

Doctor Solow checked the connections to Maddox's head. 'That programme feeds information straight into the deepest control centres of Maddox's brain. Soon we can cut into that programming, alter it. Whatever commands we give him, Maddox will have no other choice than to obey.'

The Doctor's little group had left the chemical store and was trudging along more endless white metal corridors.

Tegan was fed up with it. 'Have you *any* idea where we're going, Doctor?'

'As a matter of fact, I do, Tegan. We're making for the Bridge. Repairs to the TARDIS will take a little time. If we have to stay here for a while, we'd better get the Captain's permission.' They came to a lift. 'Aha!' said the Doctor.

Turlough studied the control panel. 'Up or down?'

'Well, if I remember correctly, the Base command centre is usually at the top of the structure.'

Before the Doctor could stop him, Turlough reached out and stabbed a control button on the panel. Immediately a light began flashing on the control panel.

The Doctor sighed. 'Really, Turlough! You see what you've done?'

'I only pressed for the lift. What's the matter?'

The Doctor indicated the light. '*This* is. There's obviously some kind of a code, so they can detect unauthorised users. It's what's called security. We'd better find someone in authority, and quickly. Come on.'

A door slid across the corridor ahead of them,

blocking their path.

'What do we do now?' asked Tegan.

'They've sealed off the area. We'd better get back to the TARDIS. We'll be safer there.'

Hurriedly the Doctor led them back along the corridor. They were in a military-style establishment, a closed environment whose inhabitants were almost certainly under considerable pressure. In such an environment, the security guards were more than likely to be trigger-happy.

Vorshak was back on the Bridge, where the atmosphere was still very tense. Recent mysterious events, combined with the practice missile-run, had left everyone edgy.

'Perimeter defence now complete, Commander,' reported Preston. She stared at her monitor screen and then exclaimed, 'Intruders, Commander! Security has detected intruders on the Base.'

'What? Where are they?'

'Area C, Commander.'

Vorshak's first thought was for the duplicate programme-disc. 'Post guards around the PS unit. Tell Controller Nilson and Doctor Solow what's happened. Any sign of an intruder and they're to destroy the programme disc immediately. Send combat teams into the area to hunt down the intruders.'

Preston moved over to a security intercom, and began issuing urgent commands. 'Battle teams eight and ten proceed to area C immediately. Suspected intruders. Team seven to PS unit . . .'

Vorshak turned to Bulic. 'What do you think?'

'An unidentified object, the destruction of the probe – and now this. Too much for coincidence.'

'I agree. We must act quickly. You and Preston take

command of the combat teams. Get them moving.'

'Right, sir. Preston, come with me.' Bulic and Preston hurried from the Bridge.

In the PS unit, Nilson spoke into the intercom. 'Message acknowledged. We'll remain alert.'

Doctor Solow was hovering over the unconscious Maddox. 'What was all that about?'

'Some kind of security alert – intruders. We'd better hurry.'

'I've almost finished . . .' She waited a moment or two longer, and then removed the terminal leads from Maddox's skull, replacing the concealing patches of skin and hair. She touched another control. The upper portion of the operating couch tilted slowly upwards, until Maddox was sitting upright.

'How do you feel, Maddox?' asked Nilson gently.

Maddox opened his eyes and stared vaguely at him.

'Fine . . . I'm fine, Controller.'

'Good. Now listen carefully . . .'

The Doctor and his companions were hurrying through the chemical store when somewhere nearby a lift door opened with an audible hiss. 'This way,' whispered the Doctor. They ducked behind a stack of chemical drums.

Guards came running into the storage area, commanded, Tegan noted, by a young woman. At least women seemed to have made a bit of progress in this unpleasant future.

The young woman glanced quickly round the storage area. 'Nothing here – let's move on.'

The guards hurried away.

The Doctor straightened up. 'That's torn it. Come on, back this way. They're between us and the TARDIS. We'll have to try to work our way around them.'

On the Silurian ship, the ice had melted away from the door of the hibernation chamber.

Tarpok checked the door. 'It is ready. We may enter now.' He touched a control and the door slid slowly open.

On the threshold, Icthar hesitated. So much depended on this moment: the restoration of the Silurian race to its former glory; the extermination of the ape-descended usurpers. The success or failure of his most cherished plans would be determined by what happened in this chamber in the next few minutes. Icthar strode into the chamber, Tarpok close behind him.

The ice chamber was dark and shadowy, lit by a green glow from the walls and floor, obscured by drifting clouds of ice-mist. It was occupied by row upon row of the creatures men called Sea Devils, marine cousins of the Silurian race. Ice-coated, motionless, they stood like statues, waiting as they had waited for thousands of years for the moment of awakening.

Icthar turned to Tarpok. 'Revive the Warriors.'

Tarpok moved to a console and operated controls. For a moment, nothing happened. Then slowly, very slowly, the green light faded, to be replaced by a warm golden glow.

Anxiously Icthar waited, observing the motionless ranks for any signs of life . . .

The Doctor and his companions came running along the corridor, and found their way blocked by a heavy metal door. There was a notice on the door:

COOLING CHAMBER
RADIATION AREA
DANGER — KEEP OUT

The Doctor promptly opened the door and dashed

inside. He found himself on a catwalk high above an enormous open-topped water tank. Steam drifted eerily over the surface of the water. The Doctor spotted a control console in the middle of the catwalk and hurried towards it. Reluctantly, Tegan and Turlough followed.

'What are we doing in here?' asked Tegan nervously.

The Doctor was busy at the console. 'You saw that notice?'

'That's why I'm asking. I don't *like* running into rooms with "Radiation – Keep Out" on the door.'

Turlough looked worriedly at the Doctor. He felt they were already in a dangerous situation, and the Doctor was very probably making it worse. 'What are you trying to *do*, Doctor?'

'Start a diversion.' The Doctor worked busily for a few moments and then straightened up. 'There, that's it.'
'What have you done?'

'Oh, just hotted things up a bit. I've set the reactor on overload.'

Tegan gasped. 'You mean it'll explode?'

'Oh, I shouldn't think so, not for several hours. They've got plenty of time to work out what I've done, and put things right again.'

'You're mad,' said Tegan flatly.

Turlough looked at the console. All kinds of dials and gauges were creeping steadily upwards, and already a warning light was flashing. No doubt there would soon be alarms going off all over the base. 'The Doctor's right. This will tie up dozens of people, keep them busy for hours.'

The Doctor smiled, pleased to be appreciated for once. 'Precisely. And in the confusion, we shall slip back to the TARDIS.'

It was a good scheme, but the timing was just a little off. As the Doctor spoke the door at the other end of the catwalk opened and two armed guards appeared.

At the sight of the three intruders, the first guard raised his blaster. Then a man in a brown uniform pushed his way through the guards and knocked down the weapon. 'No! We can't risk a shot in here.'

The Doctor heard the announcement with considerable relief. The catwalk was only wide enough for one person at a time. If he could cause a delay . . .

As the guards advanced, the Doctor turned to his companions. 'When I say run – run!' he said.

The guards came nearer, and nearer.

'Right,' shouted the Doctor. 'Run!'

Tegan and Turlough turned and ran. The Doctor stayed where he was blocking the way.

'Get them!' shouted the man in brown.

The guards broke into a run. The Doctor stayed where he was by the console, hands raised in apparent surrender. As the leading guard reached out to grab him the Doctor dropped his hands, and delivered a solid uppercut, dropping the guard in his tracks. 'So sorry,' said the Doctor with genuine regret. He turned to run. The second guard leaped over his fallen partner and winded the Doctor with a savage jab from the butt of his blaster-rifle. The Doctor gasped and doubled up, and the guard grabbed him, pressing him back against the guard rail.

All this happened very quickly. Tegan turned at the end door, and saw, to her horror, the Doctor wrestling with his attacker.

The Doctor could feel the metal of the guard rail pressing painfully into the small of his back. His opponent was very strong, and very angry . . . The guard shifted his grip. Seizing his opportunity the

39

Doctor wriggled free. The guard lashed out savagely and the blow caught the Doctor on the side of the head. Half-stunned, the Doctor pitched head first, over the rail, and into the water below. For a moment his body floated face downwards, then some unseen current caught hold of it, sucking it out of sight beneath the misty water.

Instinctively Tegan moved forwards. She was about to climb the rail when Turlough dragged her back. 'Tegan, no! There's nothing we can do.'

'We can't just leave him.'

Tegan looked up. Already the guards had recovered from their shock and were running toward them along the catwalk.

'Let's face it, Tegan,' said Turlough brutally. 'The Doctor's drowned.' And he dragged her away.

4

The Sea Devils Awake

The Doctor struggled back to full consciousness, and found himself twisting and turning under water.

A human would almost certainly have drowned. But the Doctor was not human. His Time Lord body had tremendous strength and resilience, resources far greater than those of any human body. It protected him now, sealing his lungs to preserve the little air that remained, slowing the beating of his twin hearts to conserve precious energy.

The water was warm, the Doctor realised, and it was strangely clear. Memory flooded back. He was inside the cooling system of the reactor. The Doctor looked round desperately for a way out. He had been carried some way into the cooling system, he sensed. There was little chance of regaining the surface, the pull of the unseen current was too strong. But there was a door ahead of him, in the side of the tank, a kind of hatchway with a wheel set into it. The Doctor kicked out, propelling himself towards the door.

He caught hold of the wheel and tried to turn it. It refused to budge. Summoning up all his remaining energy, the Doctor heaved again . . . It shifted, turned more easily – and the door swung open. The Doctor was swept through the hatchway into a small cramped space. Water was draining away and suddenly his head was above the surface.

Taking in great gasps of air, the Doctor looked about him. There was another hatchway ahead, with another wheel set into the door. Wearily the Doctor waded towards it.

Angry fists hammered on the other side of the heavy metal door. Beside it, a disembowelled door-coder showed a maze of multicoloured wires and shattered circuitry.

Turlough slipped his penknife back into his pocket. 'There, that should hold them for a while!' He looked at Tegan for approval.

Tegan was still too distressed to appreciate his cleverness. 'We should have tried to help the Doctor.'

'We couldn't,' said Turlough gently. 'There was nothing we could do. Come on, let's get back to the TARDIS.'

And what would they do when they got there, thought Tegan dully. Both she and Turlough had picked up a certain amount about the working of the TARDIS, but as for flying it to some particular destination . . .

Still, going back to the TARDIS was as good a plan as any. She followed Turlough down the corridor.

On the other side of the door, Bulic's guards were hammering at it in vain.

'Leave it,' ordered Bulic. 'Work your way round to the other side and get it open from there.'

The guards ran off in the other direction, and Bulic took out his communicator. 'Bulic to Bridge.'

Vorshak's voice crackled back. 'Bridge here.'

'I'm in the reactor cooling chamber, Commander. We've located the intruders. There seem to be three of them.'

'Well?'

'One was killed, drowned in the cooling tank. The other two got away.'

In the psycho-surgical unit Maddox was still stretched out on the operating couch, the terminals attached to his head. The computer was re-programming him – with a programme that had been specially modified by Doctor Solow.

The intercom unit beeped, and Nilson flicked a switch. 'Nilson here.'

'This is Commander Vorshak. The Base has been broken into. I need you here on the Bridge at once.'

'On my way, Commander.'

Nilson switched off the intercom and glanced down at Maddox. 'He's responding well. With Vorshak distracted, we may be able to activate him sooner than we expected!'

Doctor Solow was worried. 'These intruders . . . if the Eastern Bloc planned a raid, would you not have been informed?'

'Not necessarily.'

'But who *are* they?'

'That is what I intend to find out,' said Nilson calmly, and went out of the room.

Doctor Solow looked worriedly after him.

Listening to Nilson's calm lucid explanations of the logic of history, it had seemed so clear, so obvious, that only through the ideals he preached could peace and justice return to the world. Now, faced with the reality of treachery, faced with murder, deceit, the manipulation of the mind of a man too weak to resist, Doctor Solow was no longer quite so sure.

A radiation-suited guard came along the corridor and

discovered the dismantled entry-coder. He should have sent for a repair squad at once. Instead he began fiddling with the damaged unit.

There was a crackle of sparks. A surge of electricity sent him flying across the corridor. He hit the far wall with a bump, and slid unconscious to the floor – just as the Doctor came round the corner . . .

Instinctively, the Doctor ran to the fallen man and knelt beside him. He checked pulse and heartbeat and then straightened up, wincing as he rubbed his own bruised stomach. He looked down at the guard. 'You'll live, old chap. And it's an ill wind . . .'

Kneeling down, the Doctor began removing the guard's radiation-suit.

Turlough and Tegan turned a corner, and found themselves facing a group of armed guards. They turned to run. A door began sliding across the corridor, blocking their escape.

Turlough shoved Tegan through the narrowing gap. 'Go on,' he shouted. 'Save yourself.'

Tegan squeezed through just in time, and the door closed behind her.

Turlough turned to face the approaching guards.

With the endless patience of the Silurian race, Icthar, Scibus and Tarpok stood waiting throughout all the long slow process of reactivation.

For what seemed an endless time the ice-shrouded shapes stood motionless, bathed with the warm golden glow of the reactivating ray. Ice melted from great scaly limbs. Icy mists swirled and faded away, as the temperature in the chamber rose steadily. Then, at long last, the Sea Devil Warriors started to come to life.

Slowly, very slowly, they flexed their mighty limbs.

Blunt-snouted reptilian heads swung to and fro. Coldly their bulging eyes surveyed the scene around them.

The blunt round heads of the Sea Devils were simpler, more streamlined than those of their elaborately crested Silurian cousins. They lacked the third eye, the source of psychic energy that enabled some Silurians to dominate lesser races by sheer mental force. But if the Sea Devils were simpler, they were also more savage. Their innate ferocity made them terrifying opponents.

Icthar surveyed the awakening Warriors with satisfaction. It was a small group, little more than a raiding party, but it was enough.

Tarpok too was studying the awakening Warriors. 'There will be a short period of orientation, Icthar. Then they will be ready.'

'Excellent. Soon I will instruct our Warriors on the plan of attack.'

One of the Warriors, the leader, was already fully revived. He stepped forward, gazing arrogantly about him. 'I am Sauvix, Commander of Elite Group One.'

'I am Icthar, sole survivor of the Silurian Triad. These are my companions, Scibus and Tarpok.'

Awed by Icthar's rank, Sauvix raised a clawed hand in salute. 'My Warriors are yours to command.'

Icthar stood silent for a moment, savouring the moment. This was the culmination of long years of preparation. After the catastrophe in the caves, when human explosives had sealed up their underground base, Icthar and his fellow survivors had decided to re-enter hibernation. They had slept for more than a hundred years.

When they re-emerged, little had changed in the world above. The ape-primitives were a little more

45

advanced, that was all. But there had been one interesting development. The ape-primitives had developed new and ingenious weapons of destruction. They had divided into two opposing camps, and in order to continue their incessant warfare they had moved beneath the sea.

The depths of the seas were the territory of the Silurians' marine cousins, the creatures men had called Sea Devils.

Icthar brooded over these things for a very long time. Then he had evolved a Plan.

Study of ancient Silurian records had revealed the existence of a Silurian battle cruiser, buried deep beneath the polar ice-cap. The ship, its weapons and its crew were alike in hibernation, preserved from the ravages of time, awaiting the moment when they would be needed once more.

Icthar and his companions had located and re-activated the ship. They had taken over the vessel, revived its living weapon, the terrifying Myrka. And now they had successfully completed the most difficult part of the operation: the awakening of Sauvix and his Warriors – the Sea Devils.

It had been unwise of the ape-primitives to venture beneath the seas, thought Icthar. Now a terrible vengeance awaited them. It was time for them to relinquish their rule over the planet Earth, to make way for their superiors. The time of the Silurians and of the Sea Devils had come again.

Gravely Icthar raised his hand, returning Sauvix's salute. 'All is prepared, Sauvix. Follow me.'

Disguised in the still-unconscious guard's radiation-suit, which had so conviently and unexpectedly come his way, the Doctor slipped the face-concealing helmet over his head.

He wrinkled his nose in disgust. Clearly, garlic had recently featured in the menu of the Base canteen.

The Doctor looked down at the guard. 'My dear chap, what have you been eating?' he said reproachfully.

Picking up the guard's blaster-rifle, the Doctor hurried on his way.

As Nilson walked unhurriedly onto the Bridge, Vorshak was speaking on the intercom. 'Right, well done! Bring him up here right away.' He turned to Nilson. 'They've captured one of the intruders. He's being brought up here now. I'd like you to be present at the interrogation.'

'Yes, of course. Do we know who they are – or how they got in?'

'That's what I'd like you to find out.'

Tegan was running along the corridors, moving, she hoped, in the direction of the TARDIS. Suddenly a helmeted figure appeared around the corner and grabbed her by the arm. Tegan began struggling wildly until the figure pushed back the visor on its helmet to reveal the smiling face of the Doctor. Tegan hugged him delightedly. 'Doctor! I thought you were dead.'

'So did I for a moment! Where's Turlough?'

Tegan explained what had happened. 'The guards must have caught him. We've got to help him.'

'I'd better get you back to the TARDIS.'

'Oh no you don't, Doctor. I want to help find Turlough.'

'All right, all right!'

Tegan sniffed. 'What on Earth have you been eating, Doctor?'

'Never mind that, Tegan. Come along, if you're

coming!'

They hurried off.

Sauvix stood beside Icthar, watching proudly as his Warriors filed from the ice chamber.

'How soon will they be ready for combat?' asked Icthar.

'They are ready now,' said Sauvix simply. 'Battle orientation commenced automatically, the instant we revived.'

'Excellent, Sauvix.' He handed the Commander a scroll. 'Here is your plan of attack. Study it well. The ape-primitives' Base must be taken intact.'

The voice of a radiation squad technician was coming from the Bridge intercom.

'Main reactor stabilised, Commander. We now have full power again.'

Vorshak turned from the intercom, as Bulic marched into the room. Behind him, flanked by two armed guards was a thin-faced, sandy-haired young man, clearly the captured intruder. A nasty, treacherous-looking type he was too, thought Vorshak.

The prisoner was brought forward.

Nilson studied him thoughtfully. 'What is your name?'

'Turlough,' said the prisoner sulkily. 'What's yours?'

'I am Nilson. This is Commander Vorshak, senior officer of this Base. Now, I think you had better tell us how you come to be here.'

Turlough jerked his head towards Bulic. 'I've already told him . . .'

Vorshak stepped forward, looming threateningly over Turlough. 'Now listen, and listen carefully. You have a choice. Co-operate, and tell us all you know and you'll be treated honourably. Should you remain stubborn, you'll be made to co-operate, and it could be a long and painful business. So start talking.'

Turlough was very frightened and fear made him aggressive. 'I've told him and I'm trying to tell you . . . We are not enemy agents or saboteurs.'

'So why did you try to destroy the reactor?'

'That was the Doctor. There was no real damage. He only wanted to create a diversion so we could get away.'

'Do you really expect me to believe that?'

'If the Doctor had intended to destroy your reactor, it would be lying in pieces at your feet,' said Turlough arrogantly. Tact had never been his strong point.

The Doctor and Tegan turned into a short corridor that ended in a massive steel door. The Doctor nodded in satisfaction. 'Good, that must be the entrance to the Bridge. Tegan, you'd better stay here.' He bustled her into a nearby alcove.

'What in the world can I hope to achieve in here?'

'My peace of mind, for a start! Anyway, you haven't got a disguise. Please, Tegan, don't argue.' He bustled her into the alcove. 'Now, I don't need to tell you what to do if anything goes wrong!'

No, he didn't need to tell her, thought Tegan. If anything did go wrong, there was nothing she could do! 'Good luck, Doctor.'

'Thank you.' The Doctor set off.

There was the usual entry-coder by the Bridge door. The Doctor studied it, wondering if he could possibly by-pass it without setting off an alarm. His problem was simply and unexpectedly solved when the door opened and an off-duty technician hurried out.

Lowering his helmet-visor, the Doctor slipped through the open door, and it closed behind him.

Once inside, the Doctor found himself standing at the entrance to the Bridge complex. There in the middle he could see the main command console. Turlough, flanked by armed guards, was being interrogated by a number of uniformed figures.

The Doctor worked his way unobtrusively along the wall.

'The TARDIS is a kind of ship . . .' said Turlough. 'It's multi-dimensional. I know it doesn't seem to make sense but that's how we got here.'

Nilson said, 'He's insulting our intelligence, Commander. Trying to make us think he's nothing more than a lost tourist!'

'If you had nothing to hide, why didn't you declare yourselves immediately?' asked Bulic.

'We were going to – then I accidentally set off an alarm, and the Doctor said we'd better get back to the TARDIS . . .'

Vorshak turned to Nilson. 'What do you think?'

'He may be telling the truth, Commander, but I doubt it. We can't be sure without delving deeper into his mind.'

Vorshak turned away. 'Then see to it, Nilson. Delve! We must have the truth.'

Nilson nodded to Turlough's guards. 'Take him to the PS unit.'

A guard reached for Turlough's arm.

Suddenly a radiation-suited figure sprang forward, knocked the weapon from the guard's hand and jumped back, swinging a blaster-rifle in an arc to cover the little group. Instinctively Bulic reached for his hand-blaster, but the muzzle of the weapon swung round to cover him.

Pulling off his helmet, the Doctor smiled round the

50

astonished little group. 'Well, gentlemen,' he said cheerfully. 'It seems we have a problem!'

5

The Attack

Continuing her search for the third, and still unaccounted for intruder, Lieutenant Preston and her two guards came down a spiral staircase. She found herself looking at a strange square blue object, a kind of box . . .

She approached it cautiously and saw that the door was slightly ajar.

'Follow me,' she ordered. Drawing her blaster, she pushed the door open and went inside. She felt a brief moment of disorientation — then suddenly she was in an impossibly large control room, with a complex many-sided control console in the centre.

The two guards were gazing around them with dazed astonishment.

She shook her head in sheer disbelief and said weakly, 'Good heavens . . .' Looking round she noticed another door on the other side of the room. Pointing she said, 'Check through there, and report back.'

The guards crossed the control room and disappeared through the inner door.

Slowly Lieutenant Preston reached for her communicator. This would have to be reported. But — what on earth was she going to say . . .

'Perhaps I should introduce myself,' said the intruder. 'I'm the Doctor.'

Bulic was an experienced combat veteran and he knew that the newcomer's advantage was only temporary. You couldn't hold even a small group of people at blaster-point for ever.

'Your move, Doctor,' he said calmly.

'So it is. Perhaps it's time for a little mutual trust. Turlough was telling the truth, you know.' With that, the Doctor handed the blaster to the astonished Vorshak, and started climbing out of his disguise.

Bulic reached for his weapon, but Vorshak stopped him with an abrupt gesture.

There was a bleep from the intercom, and Vorshak crossed over to it. 'Vorshak here.'

Even over the intercom, Lieutenant Preston's voice sounded tense, uncertain. 'Commander, I think we've found the intruder's craft.'

'Go on,' snapped Vorshak.

'It's amazing. I don't think it can possibly come from this planet . . . it's . . . it's bigger on the inside than the outside. There's a control room, corridors, more rooms, all packed into a little blue box.'

'Is it armed?'

'Not as far as we can tell, Commander.'

Vorshak stood for a moment, considering this astonishing new information. 'Very well. Leave the craft alone. Put a guard on it, and report back to the Bridge.'

'Well, Commander?' said the Doctor gently.

Vorshak looked at Turlough. 'Multi-dimensional.' That's what the boy had said. 'It seems your friend may have been telling the truth after all.'

Icthar stood waiting on the Bridge of the Silurian ship. He showed no tenseness, no excitement, even though the plan that might well determine the fate of all his people, and of the Earth itself, was about to be put into effect.

Sauvix approached him and saluted. 'All is ready. The Warriors are armed and at their battle stations.'

'Excellent, Sauvix.' Icthar turned to his two companions. 'Scibus, Tarpok, commence the power build-up. It is time to begin.'

Clawed hands moved over the strange organic-looking controls and soon the Silurian ship began throbbing with energy, like a living being. It rose from the undersea volcano crater and slid through the murky waters, like some great predator, poised for attack . . .

Tegan was growing impatient in her hiding place. The Doctor had been on the Bridge for some little time now. Since he hadn't returned with Turlough, something had presumably gone wrong. In which case, it was up to Tegan to rescue them both.

She stepped cautiously out of her hiding place, and found herself facing a young woman and a guard, both armed.

The guard covered her with his blaster-rifle.

The young woman said politely, 'Did you want something?'

'All right, Doctor,' said Commander Vorshak. 'I'm prepared to believe that you're *not* actively hostile, despite your interference with the reactor.'

The Doctor looked rather shamefaced. 'Thank you. You're very kind.'

'But that doesn't mean I trust you completely. I should like to see a demonstration of this ship of yours.'

'Well, when I've repaired her, you'd be most . . .'

He broke off as Tegan came onto the Bridge, escorted by a woman officer and a guard.

Lieutenant Preston saluted. 'The third intruder, Commander. I found her lurking outside.'

Turlough moved to join his fellow captive. 'Are you all right?'

Tegan nodded, looking worriedly at the hostile group around them.

Suddenly the wail of an alarm filled the Bridge.

Lieutenant Karina called, 'Commander, the screen!' A cylindrical shape was registering on the main scanner screen. 'It's some kind of ship, Commander. And it's heading straight towards the Base.'

Vorshak studied the image. 'Isn't that the thing we picked up before?'

'I think it is, sir.'

Maddox called across from his console. 'We're getting a clear sensor-reading, Commander. It's a ship all right. But it's not one of ours. The readings don't correspond with any known enemy ship either.'

A terrible recognition was dawning in the Doctor's mind.

The shape on the screen continued its remorseless advance.

'Prepare to fire energy-tracers,' ordered Vorshak.

'No!' shouted the Doctor. 'You mustn't. I think I know what it is!'

Vorshak swung round. 'Are you saying you recognise that thing?'

'Yes. You mustn't attack it.'

'You're hardly in a position to give orders here, Doctor.'

'Ready to fire, Commander,' reported Bulic.

'If you open fire you'll regret it,' warned the Doctor. 'I tell you, I know what that ship is!'

'Are you telling us not to defend ourselves?'

'I'm telling you you have no defence. That's a Silurian battle cruiser.'

Vorshak stared at him. 'Silurian?'

'The race that ruled Earth before your species evolved.'

Hands poised over his weapons console, Bulic looked at Vorshak. 'Do we fire, sir?'

'Trust me, Commander,' urged the Doctor. 'Make contact with them, find out what they want.'

'It's what we want that matters, Doctor – and that's to keep them away from this Base. Bulic, open fire!'

Bulic's hands stabbed at the console. An energy-beam sped towards the intruder.

Suddenly the screen flared white with a blinding flash.

On the Bridge of the Silurian battle cruiser a gauge glowed steadily.

'The deflector is locked onto their energy-beam.' reported Scibus emotionlessly. 'Their external weapon system is now suppressed.'

Icthar's voice was equally calm. 'Proceed as planned.'

Monitor screens on the Bridge showed only a blur of static.

'Fire again!' ordered Vorshak.

Karina looked up from her console. 'The weapon systems are dead, sir.'

Vorshak glared suspiciously at the Doctor. 'You knew that would happen!'

'I did try to warn you.'

'What have they done?' asked Preston.

'It's a particle suppressor – they turned your own energy-beam back on to you. They could have blown this base apart if they'd wanted to – you certainly gave them enough reason.'

The Silurian ship glided through the depths and settled gently onto the ocean floor close to the Sea Base.

On the Bridge, Scibus reported, 'We are in position.'

'Release the Myrka,' ordered Icthar. 'Sauvix, proceed to your station. When the Myrka begins its work, you and your Warriors will commence the attack on the main entry point.'

Vorshak was desperately trying to get his demoralised Bridge crew back into action. 'I want full damage reports from everyone as soon as possible. Maddox, set the computer scan to analyse the Silurian weapon. Bulic, all guards to battle stations.'

For a moment the Doctor and his companions were forgotten in the bustle of activity.

Tegan said, 'I gather you've met these Silurians before, Doctor? When?'

'A long time ago,' said the Doctor sombrely. 'I let them down before – now it seems I'll do so again.' The Doctor was silent for a moment, remembering his previous encounters with the extraordinary reptilian species. The Silurians had evolved millions of years before man. They had developed a technologically advanced civilisation with an emphasis on bio-engineering. In addition, many of them had developed almost mystic powers.

This reptile civilisation had ruled the Earth – until their astronomers had warned them that the globe was about to be struck by a rogue planet from outer space. To escape the catastrophe, the Silurians had put themselves into deep hibernation, sealing themselves in shelters deep beneath the ground – or the seas.

The catastrophe the Silurians feared had never happened. Instead of striking the Earth the little planet had gone into orbit around it, becoming Earth's moon. The re-activating triggers had failed to work, and the Silurians had slept on, until . . .

It had all happened during his third incarnation, the Doctor recalled, the time of his exile on Earth. The energy of an underground research centre had revived a Silurian colony in a nearby cave system.

The great reptiles had awakened – only to find that Earth, their Earth, had been over-run by the apes. In the inevitable conflict that followed, the Doctor had tried to act as peacemaker. For a time it had seemed that he might succeed in convincing Silurians and Humans alike that the Earth was big enough for both of them. But in the end the extremists on both sides had triumphed. The Silurians had been entombed in their underground base.

Events had followed the same tragic pattern when the Silurians' marine cousins, the Sea Devils, had revived. This time the situation had been worsened by the meddling activities of the Doctor's old enemy, the Master. The Doctor had been forced to choose the lesser of two evils, thereby bringing about the destruction of the Sea Devils.

Turlough's voice interrupted the Doctor's reverie. 'These Silurians, Doctor – are they hostile?'

The Doctor nodded. 'They are now. But they're honourable too, in their own way. All they want is to live in peace, on a planet they consider their own.'

Silurians and humans – two warring species, thought the Doctor, so different, and yet in some ways so alike: both intelligent, aggressive, arrogant, both convinced that the Earth was theirs by right. Was there really any chance at all of making peace between them? Very little, thought the Doctor sadly. But all the same he knew he had to try.

He moved closer to Vorshak. 'Commander!'

'Yes, what is it?'

'You can't fight them, you know,' said the Doctor quietly. 'Certainly not alone.'

'I can try.'

'Inform your people on the surface. Tell them what's happening down here.'

'I can't. Things have reached crisis point up there. I've been ordered to maintain radio silence. I can't risk revealing Sea Base Four's position to the enemy.'

'East or West, friend or enemy – the distinction will be lost on the Silurians, I assure you,' said the Doctor grimly. 'To them you're all the same. Ape-descended primitives. An evolutionary error they're determined to correct.'

The intercom bleeped and an anguished voice shouted. 'Commander, there's something outside airlock one. It's trying to force the outer door!'

Vorshak swung round on Bulic. 'Get a combat team down there. Lieutenant Preston, deploy the duty guards to cover the other airlocks.'

The Doctor stepped forward. 'Let me go to airlock one. I know the Silurians. If I can talk to them, we may still be able to avoid bloodshed.'

Vorshak hesitated. 'All right, you can try. But remember, Doctor, we have no reason to trust you. Watch him closely, Bulic. At the first sign of treachery – kill him.'

Collecting guards on his way, Bulic strode off. The Doctor followed, and so did Tegan and Turlough, assuming, correctly it seemed, that Vorshak's words applied to them as well.

They arrived at airlock one to find guards already on

duty, staring nervously at an alarm light flashing above the door.

'Any change?' asked Bulic.

One of the guards shook his head. 'Nothing since we first reported.'

Suddenly there was the screech of an alarm and an instrument panel by the airlock door exploded in a shower of sparks.

Bulic said tensely. 'They've blown the magnetic locks on the outer door.'

There was a muffled clang, followed by a low, thudding, pulsing sound.

Bulic leaned forward, listening. 'They're in the airlock.'

'How can you tell?' whispered Tegan.

'Hear that noise? The automatic pumps have started up.'

'Look!' screamed Turlough. He pointed.

The massive pressure wheel on the airlock door was beginning to turn.

Lieutenant Preston's voice came from the intercom. 'I'm at airlock five, Commander. It's under attack as well.'

'Right,' snapped Vorshak. 'I'll come down. Lieutenant Karina, put all the reserve teams on combat alert. Maddox, stand by for synch-up. We may have to contact Sea Base Command after all.'

Maddox looked appalled. 'But Commander, the orders . . .'

'Perhaps the Doctor knows what he's talking about. If he does, these creatures are a threat to all mankind.'

As Vorshak ran from the Bridge, Doctor Solow entered and made her way towards Nilson, who was busy at his console. 'Nilson, we must speak.'

'All right. No need for panic.' Glancing round,

Nilson moved to her side.

'This is our opportunity, Doctor Solow. The Base is on war alert – and while Vorshak is busy, I'm in command on the Bridge.'

'You will activate Maddox?'

'Yes.'

'What about the invaders? If they manage to break in.'

'We shall neutralise the Sea Base whatever happens. With the help of Maddox we'll destroy all vital missile and communications circuitry.'

Like the true fanatic he was, Nilson was determined to carry out his mission even at the risk of his own life.

Bulic and his guards had bolted the main doors of airlock one from the inside.

Now they watched in fascinated horror as the heavy metal of the hatchway began bulging outwards under some enormous pressure.

'Take up defensive positions,' ordered Bulic.

The guards fell back a little, levelling their blaster-rifles.

'Will the door hold?' asked Tegan.

'I wouldn't count on it,' said Bulic grimly.

They waited, their eyes fixed on the distorted metal of the airlock door.

6

The Myrka

The atmosphere on the Bridge was more tense than ever. Everyone was studying monitor screens and instrument dials, waiting for more news of the mysterious attackers.

Doctor Solow and Controller Nilson watched Maddox fiddling nervously with the controls of his computer console. Unobserved by the rest of his colleagues Nilson slipped a small control-device from his pocket. It gave out a series of signals so faint and so high-pitched, that no one in the room seemed to hear them—no one but Maddox. To him the signals were loud and clear. They seemed to reverberate inside his confused and frightened brain. Maddox rose to his feet, swaying a little.

Karina glanced at him in concern. 'Maddox, are you all right?'

Maddox didn't reply.

Controller Nilson raised his voice. 'Doctor Solow, Mr Maddox is unwell. Get him off the Bridge.'

'But he's needed here,' protested Karina.

'I'm afraid he's useless in his present condition.'

Nilson nodded to Solow and she took Maddox's arm, leading him off through the door that led to the computer bay.

Worriedly, Karina watched them go. 'Shall I inform the Commander, sir?'

'No,' said Nilson quickly. 'I'll see to it. Return to your post. I'm sure Doctor Solow will have Maddox back on duty very soon.'

The door of airlock one was buckling inwards before their eyes, shaken by a series of incredibly heavy blows. It looked as if the door would give at any moment.

Bulic and his guards levelled their blasters.

The Doctor and his companions were standing a little ahead of the guards. The Doctor moved them to one side, out of the line of fire.

'Suppose these Silurians don't want to listen to you, Doctor?' asked Tegan uneasily.

The Doctor winced as the door was shaken by another tremendous thump. 'Try to look on the bright side, Tegan.'

Suddenly the top edge of the door broke away completely, crashing to the ground. A savage roar of triumph echoed through the corridor.

'It's some kind of animal,' gasped Turlough.

Part of a hideous face could be seen through the gap at the top of the door. They caught a glimpse of glowing eyes, corrugated green skin and savage fangs.

'Oh dear,' said the Doctor softly.

Tegan stared at him. 'What is it?'

'The Myrka.'

'Great,' said Turlough bitterly. 'And what's the Myrka?'

'A kind of sea dragon specially bred and adapted by the Silurians.'

'Adapted?'

'It's a kind of cyborg really – part animal, part machine. A sort of living weapon – almost invincible, I'm afraid.'

The airlock door shuddered under another tremendous blow.

The attack on airlock five was well under way by the time Vorshak arrived.

'They're inside the airlock, Commander,' reported Lieutenant Preston.

'That didn't take long.'

Vorshak studied the door.

The edge of the door seal was beginning to blacken, giving off wisps of smoke.

Lieutenant Karina was worried. Maddox had been in the computer bay for some time now. While he was absent the Base was helpless.

And why had Doctor Solow taken him to the computer bay at all? Why not give emergency first aid on the spot? That was standard procedure during an attack. Or if the problem was too serious, why not take him back to the PS unit where he could be properly treated? She looked for Controller Nilson, and saw that he was in Vorshak's command chair, studying the main monitor screen.

Karina rose and moved silently towards the computer bay. She reached the door unobserved, slipped inside – and stopped, staring in disbelief at what she saw.

A number of wall panel covers had been removed, exposing a mass of computer circuitry. Maddox was busy at one of the exposed panels, his fingers moving with almost superhuman speed, removing some circuits, transposing others, severing and re-making connections. It was quite clear that what was going on here was not repair but destruction – Maddox was rendering the computer useless – the all-important computer on which the security of the Base depended.

'Maddox, what are you doing?' she cried.

'His duty – as I dictate it,' said another voice.

It was Doctor Solow. She was watching Maddox at

his work of destruction with an air of quiet satisfaction.

'It's sabotage,' said Karina horrified. 'Stop it, Maddox. Stop it at once!'

It was as if Maddox could not hear her. He worked on at tremendous speed, face blank, as if under some kind of remote control.

Karina turned to run, to give the alarm. Nilson was blocking the doorway, a small control-device in his hands. He operated it, and it gave out faint high-pitched signals.

Immediately Maddox stopped what he was doing. He turned and came over towards Karina. His hands shot out, gripping her about the throat.

'Now kill her, Maddox!' ordered Nilson.

'No!' gasped Karina. 'No!' She struggled wildly, but Maddox seemed to have superhuman strength.

Maddox knew in some part of his mind that Karina was his friend. She had helped him, listened to his worries, tried to calm his fears. But Nilson had given the order, and for Maddox disobedience was literally impossible. As if of their own accord, his hands tightened about Karina's throat.

Nilson looked on calmly as Maddox completed his dreadful task. When it was quite clear that Karina was dead, Nilson adjusted the control device.

Immediately Maddox opened his hands, letting Karina's body drop as if it no longer existed for him. Stepping over the body, he returned to the computer circuits and resumed his task of destruction as if nothing had happened.

Doctor Solow was horrified. 'What are we going to do?' she sobbed.

'We are going to remain calm,' said Nilson icily.

'But once the body is discovered . . .'

'The body isn't going to be discovered. You're going

to hide it, somewhere in here. Maddox will be finished before very long.'

'What happens then?'

'To Maddox? He will be of no further use to us. Perhaps they'll execute him for Karina's murder.'

'What happens to us? The Base is under attack, remember.'

'That doesn't concern us either,' said Nilson calmly. 'Remember our mission. Once this Base has been rendered helpless, unable to fire its proton missiles, we shall leave.'

'How?'

'In the escape pod. I already have the activation keys and departure codings in my possession. An East Bloc cruiser is waiting to pick us up.' His voice hardened. 'Now pull yourself together, Doctor Solow. Find a place to hide that body and keep an eye on Maddox. See that no one distracts him from his task. I must return to the Bridge.' Calm and self-possessed as ever, Nilson strode from the computer bay.

Doctor Solow caught Karina's body under the arms and began dragging it across the room. It was strange, she thought. With all her medical experience, she hadn't realised that a dead body could be so heavy . . .

The gap in the doorway of airlock one was larger now, and more of the creature's terrifying head and body could be seen.

'Take aim,' yelled Bulic. 'Fire!'

There was a crackle of energy. At least one of the blaster bolts struck the Myrka squarely on the forehead. It recoiled from the gap with a scream of rage. Seconds later the attack on the door recommenced with renewed fury.

The Doctor sighed. 'I'm afraid it takes quite a lot to impress the Myrka.'

Bulic and his men edged closer. When the Myrka appeared once more framed in the jagged gap, Bulic shouted, 'Fire!'

More energy bolts poured through the gap. There was another roar from the monster, and then silence.

'We hit it!' shouted Bulic exultantly.

Turlough gave a sigh of relief. 'You must have killed it!'

Suddenly there was another tremendous thump. Torn from its hinges, the airlock door crashed inwards against the wall scattering Bulic's men – and trapping Tegan, who was nearest, underneath it.

The Doctor ran to help her. 'Tegan, are you hurt?' He tried to pull her free. 'Are you all right?'

'I'm fine, Doctor. But I can't seem to move my leg . . .'

The Doctor looked. Tegan's body was unhurt, jammed in the angle between the door and the corridor wall. By a kind of freak accident her foot, although uncrushed, was trapped by the fallen door and she couldn't pull it free.

The Doctor glanced up at the Myrka. The bulk of its body was visible now. It was like a kind of pocket dinosaur, moving on huge back legs with smaller but still powerful limbs in front of it, a hideous dragon-like head, and a long tail. For a moment it stood waiting, surveying the scene before it.

'Fire!' shouted Bulic. 'Fire again!'

A hail of energy bolts poured through the shattered doorway. The Myrka roared, more in anger than pain. It was quite unhurt.

The Doctor resumed his efforts to free Tegan. 'How do you feel?'

'How would you feel if a door had fallen on you?

The Doctor heaved at the door. It shifted a little – but only a very little.

'Turlough, help me!'

A little reluctantly, Turlough came to help. They both tugged at the door. Even their combined efforts seemed to shift it only fractionally.

'It's no good,' gasped Turlough. 'We can't lift it . . .'

The Myrka was still framed in the airlock doorway. It seemed unhurt and it made no move to advance – but it wasn't retreating either.

'Fire again!' shouted Bulic. 'Close the range.'

Still firing, the guards advanced on the Myrka.

The Doctor looked up and saw what was happening. 'Keep back,' he shouted. 'Don't get too close – and don't let it touch you.'

The warning came too late. The leading guard moved nearer – and suddenly the Myrka lashed out. There was a fierce crackle and the man was flung back across the corridor.

He writhed for a moment, his body glowing with electrical energy, and then fell dead. The Myrka struck again and another guard died.

'Don't fire any more, it's useless,' yelled the Doctor. 'Get your people out of here.'

Bulic raised his voice. 'Clear the airlock!'

The guards began falling back.

'You too, Turlough,' ordered the Doctor.

'But what about Tegan?'

'I'll look after Tegan. Now, get out!'

Turlough fell back with the others.

'You go as well, Doctor,' gasped Tegan.

'No. I'm not leaving you. Now, I'll lift, you pull!'

The Doctor heaved at the door, while Tegan struggled to pull her foot free.

It moved a little, and then jammed again.

'You go as well, Doctor. No point in us both dying.'

'Who's talking about dying?' said the Doctor

cheerfully, and heaved again at the door.

Luckily the Myra showed no sign of leaving the airlock. It stood poised, its great dragon-like head swaying to and fro, as if surveying the scene of its victory.

Curious that electrical effect, thought the Doctor. Somehow the Silurians had engineered the thing so that its body contained a massive electric charge that could be discharged at will – a sort of cross between a dinosaur and an electric eel.

The Doctor paused, considering the problem. Fortunately Tegan's foot was only trapped, not mangled. It only needed the door to shift a very little more and she would be able to pull free. The Doctor thought about various alternative plans: some kind of grease or oil perhaps.

No time . . . The Myrka roared.

'Hurry, Doctor,' urged Tegan. 'That thing's getting restless. It's starting to edge its way out of the airlock.'

The Myrka roared again.

The Doctor redoubled his efforts.

By now Bulic's men had pulled back beyond the bulkhead area, and Turlough was swept along with them. One of the crew thrust something into his hand. 'Here!' It was a blaster-rifle dropped by one of the dead guards.

'Thanks,' said Turlough a little dubiously.

He moved closer to Bulic, who was speaking urgently into his portable communicator, reporting to Vorshak. 'The creature's already in, sir,' he was saying. 'I'm afraid our weapons seem to be useless against it.'

'Use grenades!' ordered Vorshak.

'We can't, sir. The Doctor and the girl are too close. They're trapped by the airlock.'

'Has the creature passed beyond the main bulkhead

door?'

'No sir. It's still in the airlock.'

'Then close the door. Seal off the bulkhead immediately.'

To close the bulkhead would cut off the Doctor and Tegan's only possible escape route.

'No!' shouted Turlough instinctively.

Vorshak's voice said angrily, 'Who's that? What do you mean, no? The safety of the Base depends on it. Do it, Bulic. That's an order.'

Bulic looked helplessly at Turlough. 'I'm sorry.' He moved towards a wall control panel.

'No, wait!' shouted Turlough. He tried to push Bulic away, but a shoulder-charge from a burly guard sent him flying.

Bulic stabbed at the control panel and the massive bulkhead door began to close.

The Doctor glanced over his shoulder. 'They're closing the bulkhead! Come on, Tegan, one more try!'

There was immense strength in the Doctor's relatively slight frame. Summoning all his inner resources he gave one enormous heave. At the same time the Myrka started to advance. One of its huge feet stepped on the edge of the door which raised the end that had been trapping Tegan's foot a few inches. At the same time Tegan pulled back on her foot until it felt as if it would come off – and suddenly she was free.

'Thank you so much,' said the Doctor to the Myrka.

The Doctor grabbed Tegan's hand and pulled her towards the fast-closing bulkhead door.

He was just too late. The final struggle had taken just a few seconds too long, and they reached the bulkhead door just as it slammed closed before them, cutting off their retreat.

The Doctor and Tegan turned – in time to see the

Myrka step over the fallen door and out of the airlock. It stood quite still for a moment, then it began moving towards them.

'Brave heart, Tegan,' whispered the Doctor.

Tegan was almost too indignant to be afraid. 'Brave heart?' she said incredulously. 'Brave heart? Doctor, that thing is going to kill us!'

7

The Breakthrough

Turlough picked himself up, the blaster-rifle still in his hand. He levelled it at Bulic's head. 'Open that bulkhead door!'

'I can't,' said Bulic calmly. 'Not even if I wanted to. The controls are locked now. It can only be opened from the Bridge.'

Turlough glared wildly at him, not sure if Bulic was lying or not, and almost angry enough to shoot him down anyway. Then he whirled round, and ran off down the corridor.

A guard made to follow him, but Bulic held the man back. 'Let him go,' he said, not unsympathetically. 'Sergeant, stay here on guard, I must see the Commander. The rest of you, follow me.'

The Myrka advanced.

Instinctively the Doctor stepped back, half stumbling over something on the ground. He looked down. It was a blaster-rifle dropped by one of the dead guards. The Doctor picked it up, and examined it thoughtfully.

'That won't do you much good,' said Tegan.

The Doctor's hands were busy with the rifle, extracting a gleaming black cylinder from the butt.

'Get ready, Tegan!' he said.

The Myrka was very close now. It was poised, coiled as if to spring.

'Cover your eyes!' shouted the Doctor.

Obediently Tegan threw her arm over her face.

The Doctor bowled the cylinder like a cricket ball, striking the monster right between the eyes. He closed his own eyes tightly, and sensed rather than saw the blinding flash that followed.

The Myrka reeled back, roaring and crashing against the steel wall of the corridor.

Tegan opened her eyes. 'What did you do to it?'

'Simple enough,' said the Doctor opening his eyes. 'The Myrka's body carries a charge of electricity. It exploded the blaster's power-pack.'

'So it's blinded?'

The Myrka was swinging its great head to and fro, as if trying to locate them. Once the effect of the flash faded . . .

'Temporarily,' said the Doctor.

Turlough hared along corridors, up staircases and through the now-open door to the Bridge. Guards and technicians alike were distracted by the drama of the attack, and before anyone realised what was happening, Turlough was at Nilson's side.

'The master control to bulkhead one – where is it?'

Nilson stared at him in astonishment. 'Right here. But the Commander's orders are to keep that bulkhead closed.'

Turlough covered him with his blaster-rifle. 'I know what the Commander's orders are. Now I'm giving you mine: open that bulkhead, or I'll kill you.'

Nilson stared at him for a moment.

Wild-eyed and panting, Turlough looked quite capable of carrying out his threat.

Nilson had no wish to die in defence of the Base he was working to destroy. 'Very well.'

He operated the controls.

The Myrka, recovered by now, had resumed its advance on Tegan and the Doctor. They retreated till there was nowhere else to go, until their backs were pressed against the bulkhead door. There was a sudden hiss of hydraulic power and the door began to open . . .

The moment the gap was wide enough, the Doctor shoved Tegan through, squeezing himself through after her. They pushed past Bulic's astonished sergeant, still waiting on guard. At the sight of the Myrka looming in the widening gap, the sergeant sprang forwards, raising his blaster.

'Look out!' shouted the Doctor, but it was too late. The Myrka lashed out, the sergeant's body glowed and he fell dead to the ground.

The thick bulkhead door stopped moving. It reversed its direction, starting to close again. With an angry roar, the Myrka flung itself forwards, trying to widen the narrowing gap. There was a screech of protest and the door juddered to a halt, the mechanism jammed. There was still a gap, though fortunately it was too small for the Myrka to pass through. Again the Myrka roared, hurling its weight against the edge of the door in an attempt to force it open.

It was an interesting contest, thought the Doctor – monster against machinery – but he didn't think he'd wait for the result. Grabbing Tegan's hand, he dragged her along the corridor.

On the Bridge, Nilson was stabbing frantically at the door controls. 'The hydraulic valves have blown!'

Turlough gave him a suspicious look. 'The bulkhead opened though?'

'It opened all right. But I'm not so sure it closed.'

Turlough was thinking hard. There was some hope that the Doctor and Tegan had escaped from the airlock. But if the door hadn't closed behind them, the monster would still be on their heels.

Surprising himself by his own bravery, Turlough turned and ran from the Bridge.

A quick examination had shown the Doctor that Tegan's ankle wasn't seriously hurt. But it was badly bruised, and her limp slowed their progress along the corridor.

'What will you do if the Myrka manages to break through?' she asked.

'Try to stop it before it does too much damage.'

Tegan stopped to rest for a moment, rubbing her ankle. 'That thing's practically indestructible, you said so yourself.'

'True enough, Tegan. But we all have our Achilles' heel – and that includes the Myrka. Can you go on now? I've got to talk to Commander Vorshak.'

Doctor Solow came onto the Bridge, and caught Nilson's eye. After a moment, he moved unobtrusively towards her.

'Well?'

'I've hidden Karina's body in an empty locker in the computer bay,' she whispered. 'It shouldn't be found for quite a while.' Her voice was dull, almost lifeless. By now Doctor Solow was becoming used to murder and treachery.

Nilson gave her an encouraging pat on the shoulder. 'Well done. The escape pod is ready for us. We can leave as soon as Maddox finishes his work.' He moved back towards the command console.

With a final titanic heave, the Myrka forced the door back, just far enough for its giant body to pass through. It set off down the corridor. Panic spread through the Base at the news of its coming.

Turning the corner, the Myrka overtook a fleeing crowd of Base technicians. Some ran desperately on. Others flattened themselves against the wall hoping the Myrka would pass them by. It passed, but as it did so its tail lashed to and fro, sending out great surges of electrical power. Bodies glowed and twisted and fell dead behind it.

The Myrka moved on, impervious to the terror it inspired all around.

On the Silurian ship, its progress was monitored with quiet satisfaction. The Myrka had been, so to speak, part of the equipment of the Silurian battle-cruiser. A product of Silurian genetic engineering, it had been designed as a weapon of terror and destruction. Almost as much machine as animal, it was completely under the control of its Silurian masters. Its enormous strength enabled it to smash through steel walls and the hulls of ships. The electric charge carried by the massive body repelled the effect of energy-weapons, and killed most living beings at a touch.

Like the Sea Devils, the Myrka had lain in hibernation for millions of years. Reviving it and restoring it to its deadly function had been a long and difficult task. It was gratifying to see how successfully this had been achieved.

'The Myrka has broken through the bulkhead door, Icthar,' reported Scibus. 'It is advancing through the Base. The ape-primitives are powerless.'

'Very well. Command the Myrka to make directly

for its objective. Inform Sauvix that it is imperative that he gains entry without delay.' He swung round to Tarpok. 'Is the Manipulator ready?'

Tarpok was checking over a complex piece of Silurian equipment. 'Yes, Icthar. It is now fully charged.'

'Good. Now we must prepare to join our forces in the Sea Base. Scibus, you will inform Icthar that we are coming.'

Commander Vorshak, Lieutenant Bulic and Preston and a tense group of guards were waiting by the door to airlock five.

Vorshak was listening to Nilson's report over the intercom. 'I'm afraid the creature has broken through into the Base, Commander. The boy Turlough forced us to open the bulkhead door. Somehow the creature was able to stop it from closing again.'

'Sound the alarm. I want all non-essential personnel into the bunkers right away.' Switching off the communicator, Vorshak turned to Bulic. 'Get some of your best combat-guards to airlock one immediately. We've got to stop that thing.'

'How?' protested Bulic. 'Our weapons don't seem to affect it.'

'We've got to try!'

'He's right, you know, Commander,' said the Doctor's voice. 'Your weapons are useless against the Myrka.'

Vorshak swung round. The Doctor and Tegan were hurrying towards him.

Vorshak's hand went to his blaster. 'Our weapons may not work on that creature, but they'll work on you. Do you know what your friend Turlough has done? He made Nilson open the bulkhead door, and let the monster loose in this Base.'

'He saved our lives,' said Tegan angrily.

'I ordered that bulkhead door to be kept closed, to protect the Base.'

'Leaving us in there to die!'

'It was only a matter of time, you know,' said the Doctor gently. 'Even that bulkhead door wouldn't have kept the Myrka out for very much longer.'

Lieutenant Preston had been keeping an eye on the airlock door. The line of charred metal ran most of the way around the door by now. 'I think the door-seals are about to blow, Commander,' she called.

Caught between two dangers, Vorshak stood frowning, locked in indecision.

'You'll have to handle things here,' said the Doctor. 'But if it's any consolation, I just may know how to stop the Myrka for you.'

'If I want your help I'll ask for it,' snarled Vorshak. He gave an anguished glance at the smoke-wreathed door.

'Listen,' said the Doctor quietly. 'You'll have a battle on your hands in just a moment. Do you want the Myrka coming up behind you? Let me try. What have you got to lose?'

Vorshak glared mistrustfully at him. 'I ought to have you shot.'

'Yes, yes,' said the Doctor impatiently. 'Hung, drawn and quartered as well if you like – after I've stopped the Myrka.'

'All right,' said Vorshak reluctantly. 'But I can't spare you any men, I need them all here.'

'I don't want any men. All I need is someone with some authority, someone who can get things done.'

'Lieutenant Preston, you go with him,' ordered Vorshak.

'Yes, sir. Any special orders?'

'Yes. If he gives you any more trouble, kill him.

That's an order.'

'How very encouraging,' murmured the Doctor. 'Come on!'

The Doctor, Tegan and Preston moved away, and Vorshak turned back to his men. 'Get ready, all of you – they'll be through any moment now.'

Vorshak was right. Seconds later the airlock door collapsed inwards.

Vorshak and his men stared in unbelieving horror at the terrifying figure in the doorway. Man-shaped, immensely tall, with tough corrugated skin, a reptilian-snouted head and great staring eyes, the creature wore some kind of armoured jerkin. One clawed hand help up a circular torch-like device. Behind this first apparition there were still more of the creatures, crowding into the airlock.

Vorshak recovered from his shock. 'Fire!' he shouted.

The guards opened fire. A sizzling of blaster-bolts filled the corridor.

A ray of light sprang from the device in the creature's hand. Beside Vorshak a guard screamed, twisted and died. Remorselessly, Sauvix and his Sea Devil Warriors advanced out of the airlock.

It very soon became apparent that the invaders had the upper hand. The strange circular weapons they carried killed instantly, while their armoured jerkins absorbed the blaster-fire of the guards.

'Aim for the head!' shouted Bulic. 'The head or the legs.'

The more cool-headed of his men followed his advice, and here and there a Sea Devil fell dead or wounded. But for the most part it was the humans who died. Gradually, inevitably, the guards were driven back.

In a distant corridor, Turlough heard the sizzle of blaster-fire and began running, for once, towards the sound of battle.

Finally, covered by the concentrated fire of the survivors, Bulic operated the door-controls and then sprang back behind the bulkhead with the others. Immediately the massive metal door began sliding across the corridor. The defenders concentrated their blaster-fire into the narrowing gap, forcing the Sea Devils back long enough for the door to close.

Bulic leaned wearily against the wall. 'It's no good, Commander, they've got us outgunned.'

'I know. Now it all depends on whether that bulkhead door can hold them.'

On the other side of the bulkhead, two of the Sea Devils were bringing up a bulbous-headed device, a kind of portable electronic cannon. At a gesture from Sauvix, they switched on the device and trained it on the door.

There was a steady hum of power. Slowly, very slowly, the surface of the massive metal bulkhead began to char and crumble.

For the moment at least there was no sign of this on the other side. Vorshak and his men were able to snatch a few moments of much-needed rest. Medics appeared to tend the wounded, emergency rations were issued – and suddenly Turlough came running up, blaster-rifle in hand.

'The Doctor and Tegan . . .' he gasped. 'Where are they?'

Vorshak looked grimly at him. 'So, there you are.'

Turlough had an uneasy feeling that the Commander was wondering whether to have him shot now or wait till later.

'Your friends are alive,' said Vorshak at last. 'At least for the moment. The Doctor's gone off to see if he can do something to stop this Myrka creature.' Vorshak smiled grimly. 'You might say that the Doctor is contributing to the defence of the Base – just as you are.'

'I'm sorry?' said Turlough politely.

'You are volunteering your services to defend this bulkhead. Isn't he, Bulic?'

Bulic nodded, his face grim. 'That's right. We appreciate it very much. Now – get over there with those guards – in the front!'

Turlough looked at them in horror. He'd been acting with unusual bravery – but only to try and help the Doctor and Tegan. The last thing he'd ever wanted was a hero's death. But it looked as if he was going to get one all the same.

8

Sabotage

Lieutenant Preston was following the Doctor and Tegan along the corridor when there came a bleep from her communicator. She stopped to answer it. 'Lieutenant Preston here.'

The strained voice of a guard came over the intercom. 'The monster – it's in corridor seven.'

'Try to hold it back as long as you can.'

'We'll do our best,' said the voice dubiously. 'But I wouldn't bank on it!'

The intercom flicked off.

The Doctor paused, trying to chart the Myrka's progress from his sketchy knowledge of the layout of the Base. 'It entered by airlock one, now it's in corridor seven. It must be making for somewhere . . .'

'It seems to be heading for the Bridge,' said Preston.

'Yes, that would be it. The Bridge!'

Lieutenant Preston reached for her communicator. 'I must warn them . . .'

'Later,' said the Doctor impatiently. 'Listen, do you have ultra-violet convertors on the Base?'

'Yes, I should think so. There are some in the Solarium.'

The Solarium was one of the Base's recreational facilities, a cunningly designed area where you could lounge beneath plastic palm trees on a simulated beach, against a back projection of tropical sea and sky – bathed, of course, in artificial sunshine. It was designed to counteract the effect of long spells of undersea duty. It was said you could even get a tan if you stayed in there long enough, though few people bothered.

The Doctor was thinking hard. 'Good. Now, will the Myrka need to pass this way on its route to the Bridge?'

'From corridor seven? Yes, this is the main access corridor.'

'Perfect. I'll need the ultra-violet convertor brought here – immediately please.'

Giving him a puzzled look, Preston switched on her communicator. 'Lieutenant Preston to tech. unit. Send a squad to the Solarium, dismantle the UV convertor and bring it to the junction of corridor one and the main access corridor. This is an emergency, priority one.'

The edges of the bulkhead door were charring and smoking like burnt toast, thought Turlough. Nostalgically he remembered the ritual of study-teas at his public school, with a terrified fag to make the toast. He looked at the blaster in his hand and wondered what he was doing here.

Bulic stared at the bulkhead. 'It won't hold much longer.'

Vorshak was deep in thought. 'There's only one thing for it. We'll have to break radio silence, call Sea Base Command and ask for help. We need more men, heavier weapons . . . But if we do break silence –'

'Every enemy listening post will pinpoint our position,' completed Bulic.

'It seems we lose either way. But there's no

alternative. The way things are going, this Base could fall into those creatures' hands. Our people have got to know!'

On the other side of the door, Vorshak's opposite number, Sauvix, Commander of the Sea Devils, watched the operation of the heat cannon with quiet satisfaction.

The cannon was one of the most impressive achievements of Silurian technology. It built up and focused an incredibly powerful heat-ray. The bulkhead door was made of specially reinforced steel, several feet thick. Under the influence of the heat cannon, it was crumbling like the wall of a sandcastle attacked by incoming waves.

Sauvix looked around his Warriors. They stood grouped around the door waiting. It would not be long now.

A couple of technicians came staggering along the corridor carrying the UV convertor, a bulky silver box packed with electronic equipment.

'There you are,' said the Doctor. 'Just set it up over here, would you? And if you'd be kind enough to lend me that tool kit?'

Unclipping the tool kit from his belt, the technician handed it to the Doctor.

'That will be all,' said Lieutenant Preston.

'Ma'am.' The technician saluted and hurried away, glad to be gone.

The Doctor removed the cover from an electrical junction box and began connecting up the UV convertor. He looked up at Lieutenant Preston. 'What do you think? Will the lighting circuit bear the maximum convertor load?'

She shrugged. 'Just about! I'd better keep watch.'

She moved along the corridor, keeping an eye out for the Myrka.

Tegan watched the Doctor for a moment. 'What does that thing do?'

'Converts normal lighting into ultra-violet.'

'What are you planning to do with it?'

'Oh, I just want to bring a little sunshine into the Myrka's life!'

Tegan gave him one of her long-suffering looks.

The guards were doing their best to delay the Myrka, but there was little hope of success.

Some of them tried the Doctor's trick of throwing power packs at the monster, but the trick wouldn't work for a second time. The Myrka was well aware of the danger by now. It turned its head, smashing aside the power-packs with claws or tail, so that they exploded harmlessly away from its eyes. The guards could only fire their useless weapons and fall back as slowly as possible. Many died in the process, electrocuted by the energy field that crackled through the Myrka's body.

The Myrka continued its relentless progress towards the Bridge.

Controller Nilson was listening to Bulic's voice on the communicator. 'The Commander is on his way up to signal Sea Base Command. Have Maddox stand by for link-up.'

Like the firing of the missiles, direct communication with Sea Base Command was a process that could be authorised by the Commander alone. As a further precaution, it could only be done by computer link-up with an authorised synch-operator.

Doctor Solow gave Nilson an anxious look. With Maddox in his current condition, the work of sabotage still not complete, Vorshak's decision meant that they both risked discovery.

'What are we going to do?' she whispered.

Nilson considered the crisis with his usual icy calm. 'Maddox must finish the work that he has started,' he said with determination. 'Come with me.'

They moved towards the computer bay.

Lieutenant Preston was scanning the corridor ahead for signs of the Myrka. She turned and looked over her shoulder at the Doctor who was elbow-deep in electronic circuitry. 'I suppose you know what you're doing, Doctor?'

'The Myrka is a creature of the blackest depths,' said the Doctor thoughtfully. 'At least, it was until the Silurians started tinkering about with its biology. Anyway, it still has little tolerance of light and, I hope, none at all to ultra-violet rays.'

'Hope?' said Tegan suspiciously. 'Doctor, can you be sure this will work?'

'No, Tegan,' said the Doctor irritably. 'I can't give you any guarantees. Perhaps you'd prefer to ask it nicely to go away?'

Tegan sighed and shut up.

Maddox was still working at the same frantic speed when Nilson and Solow came into the computer bay.

Nilson nodded approvingly. 'The work goes well. He is almost finished. Doctor Solow, make your way to the escape pod and wait for me. I'll join you as soon as I can.'

'What about Maddox's conditioning tape?'

'Take it with you. It will provide our East Bloc colleagues with essential information.'

Doctor Solow nodded. 'As you wish,' she said wearily. 'Good luck.' Taking the disc from a locker drawer she hurried away, clutching it in her hand.

The Doctor was connecting circuits with desperate speed.

'Are you ready, Doctor?' called Preston.

Absorbed in his work, the Doctor didn't answer.

'Doctor,' said Tegan urgently. 'Are you ready yet?'

'Almost,' said the Doctor. 'Almost!' He went on with his work.

Doctor Solow came running down the corridor from the direction of the Bridge. She halted for a moment at the sight of the Doctor and Tegan, then ran on past them. The Doctor didn't even notice.

Tegan stared after Doctor Solow. 'Where's she off to in such a hurry?'

Lieutenant Preston looked up in surprise as Doctor Solow ran past her. 'Doctor Solow, come back,' she called. 'You mustn't go that way, it's too dangerous. The Myrka is coming . . .'

Doctor Solow ignored her. She ran round the corner, down more endless corridors, turned another corner – and found herself facing the Myrka. It was too late to turn and run, and she flung herself forward, kicking out at the Myrka in an attempt to force her way past.

The attempt was doomed. The long tail lashed out and she was thrown across the corridor, her body glowing and crackling with energy. As she slumped dead to the ground, the programme disc rolled from her outstretched hand.

The Myrka moved on.

Minutes later a guard ran from the side corridor, pausing at the sight of Doctor Solow's body. He knelt by it for a moment, checking that she was dead. As he straightened up, his eye was caught by the programme disc lying against the wall. He bent to pick it up, studying the code stamped on the case. His eyes widened. '43Y?' It was the highest security classification on the Base.

Slipping the disc in his pocket, he turned and ran back down the corridor.

As Icthar and his two fellow Silurians strode from the airlock, Sauvix and his Warriors raised their hands in salute. Icthar bowed his head, acknowledging the tribute.

'How goes the battle?' he asked.

'The outcome is certain,' said Sauvix proudly. 'The ape-primitives are no match for my Warriors. They will soon be crushed.'

Commander Vorshak hurried along on his way to the Bridge and stopped in astonishment at the sight of the Doctor.

'How is it going, Doctor? Do you have everything you need?'

'Oh yes, I think so,' said the Doctor cheerfully. 'It'll work, or it won't. We'll soon know. What's happened to Turlough, Commander?'

'He is with Bulic, helping to defend airlock five. I've decided to take your advice, Doctor, and call Sea Base Command for help!'

'Very wise,' said the Doctor drily. 'I hope it won't be too late.'

A frantic guard came running up to them. At the sight of the Commander he came to a sudden halt, giving a hasty salute. 'The monster's on its way, sir. It has already killed Doctor Solow. I found this by her body.'

Vorshak stared at the programme disc in astonishment.

The Doctor registered his reaction. 'Something

wrong, Commander?'

'I hope not, Doctor. I'm not sure.' Vorshak slipped the disc into his pocket. 'All right, I'll deal with it. Make your way to airlock five and report to Lieutenant Bulic. Lieutenant Preston, come with me to the Bridge.'

His communicator bleeped, and they all heard the panic in Bulic's voice. 'Commander Vorshak? They're in, sir. The Sea Devils have broken through. They're everywhere.'

'Do your best to hold them, Bulic. I'm on my way to the Bridge to call Sea Base Command for help.'

The corridor by airlock five was filled with the sizzling of blaster-fire.

Bulic was shouting into the communicator. 'We'll try to hold them, Commander.'

'Do what you can. You've got to buy us some time.'

Bulic raised his voice. 'Back, all of you. Move back – but as slowly as you can. We've got to delay them.'

Like the rest of the guards, Turlough fired and fell back, fired and fell back, retreating before the terrifying figures that stalked down the corridor. He took careful aim and shot the nearest Sea Devil squarely between the bulging eyes. With grim satisfaction, he saw it stagger and fall.

Fire and fall back. Fire and fall back. Too busy to be frightened, Turlough fought the desperate rearguard action with the rest.

Nilson stood in the doorway of the computer bay, watching Maddox at work.

Maddox was a ghastly sight. Face sweating, eyes staring, he seemed on the point of collapse, yet he worked on with abrupt, galvanic movements, as if plugged in to some invisible power source.

Nilson studied him thoughtfully. 'Don't die on me, Maddox, not yet! Not till you have served your purpose.'

He took the control device from his pocket. 'Hurry, Maddox, there isn't much time!' He switched the control to a higher frequency.

Maddox began working even more quickly, his movements swift and jerky like someone in a speeded up film.

Nilson knew that Maddox could not last much longer at this pace. Soon he would simply burn out. But what did it matter, as long as his task was completed . . .

Icthar and his companions listened impassively to Sauvix's report. 'The ape-primitives are in full retreat. Most of the strategic areas are already under our control.'

'That is excellent news,' said Icthar gravely.

'Soon the Myrka will take the Bridge. When that is done, the outcome is certain.'

Vorshak strode onto the Bridge and tossed the programming disc onto the console in front of Nilson. 'Maddox's conditioning disc. You were ordered to guard it carefully, to return it to me when you had finished. Well?'

Nilson's astonishment was quite genuine. How on earth had Vorshak come by the disc? 'Doctor Solow had charge of the disc. I assumed she had already returned it to you. Has something happened –'

'Doctor Solow is dead, killed by the Myrka. Where's Maddox?'

'In the computer bay, checking on the synch circuitry.'

Vorshak turned to Preston. 'Get him in here!'

Lieutenant Preston went over to the door of the computer bay, opened it, and stood staring in horror at what she saw. 'Commander, come quickly!'

Vorshak ran to the door, and looked inside.

The place was a shambles, panels removed from the computer banks, whole areas of circuitry dismantled. Maddox was still dismantling computer circuitry at the same incredible speed.

'Maddox,' roared Vorshak. 'What are you doing?' He dashed up to Maddox and tried to pull him away from the computer.

Vorshak was a big man and exceptionally strong. Maddox was frail by comparison. Yet Maddox grabbed Vorshak and hurled him across the room like a child, then turned back to his work of destruction. Picking himself up, Vorshak returned to the attack. Once again he was thrown aside with the same careless ease.

Nilson appeared in the doorway and stood watching impassively. As Vorshak was about to attack for the third time, Nilson jabbed at the controls of the device hidden in his pocket.

Immediately Maddox went rigid, hands clawing at his temples. He swayed for a moment and then fell.

Preston knelt beside him feeling his pulse. 'He's still alive.'

Vorshak was staring grimly around the computer room. 'Never mind about Maddox. Check the damage to the computer!'

The Doctor and Tegan waited tensely beside the UV convertor. They could hear shouts and screams, the sizzle of blaster-fire and the angry roars of the Myrka. The sounds had been getting louder for some time, and now they were very close.

The Doctor looked at Tegan. 'Well, here it comes.

91

Pretty soon we'll know if my theory is correct!'

There was a deafening roar, and the Myrka appeared around the corner. It paused for a moment at the sight of the Doctor and Tegan. The terrifying dragon-like head swung round, and the red eyes glared threateningly at the Doctor.

Almost as if it recognised him, the Myrka gave a challenging roar and advanced towards them.

9

The Hostage

Tegan cowered back as the monster advanced. 'Switch that thing on, Doctor. Switch it on *now*!'

'Just a few more feet,' said the Doctor softly.

The Myrka came closer and closer, until it was almost upon them. Just as it seemed that the great tail must lash round and destroy them – the Doctor threw the convertor switch.

'Cover your eyes, Tegan,' he shouted.

Suddenly the corridor lighting turned to a glaring white ultra-violet light.

The Myrka jerked to a halt. It writhed in agony for a moment and then toppled over sideways, landing with a thud that shook the corridor. It lay twitching, steam rising from its body. A final convulsive jerk, and it was still.

Cautiously Tegan moved closer. 'Is it dead?'

'Very,' said the Doctor with satisfaction. 'Let's get back to the Bridge.'

An instrument on Tarpok's belt gave an alarm signal. He took it out and studied it for a moment. 'The life-force of the Myrka does not register, Icthar. It has been destroyed.'

'The ape-primitives are more cunning than we had

thought. Sauvix, divert your Warriors. They must capture the Bridge without delay.'

Sauvix saluted. 'At once, Icthar.'

Vorshak looked round the wrecked computer bay, down at the unconscious body of Maddox and then at Nilson. His voice was cold and furious. '*You* were in charge of the Bridge, Nilson. How could you *not* know what was going on here?'

Nilson made no reply.

Lieutenant Preston opened a locker. She recoiled in horror at the huddled shape within. 'It's Karina, Commander. She's dead – strangled . . .'

Vorshak's face hardened. 'I don't know what's been going on here, Nilson, though I shall find out. But you're responsible and, I promise you, you'll answer to a court martial. First you're going to revive Maddox and re-condition him. I want him ready for synch-up as soon as possible. I'm going to signal Sea Base Command.'

Nilson shook his head. 'I'm afraid I can't do that, Commander.'

'You'll do it all right –' Vorshak broke off. Nilson was covering him with a pocket-blaster.

'Your weapon please, Commander,' said Nilson calmly. 'Yours too, Lieutenant.' Nilson waved his blaster. 'Now, back to the Bridge.'

Helplessly they obeyed.

'What exactly do the Silurians want, Doctor?' asked Tegan.

'Oh, that's obvious, surely. Control a Base like this with its proton missiles and you can control the Earth.'

'Or destroy it?'

'Very probably.'

They carried on down the corridor, heading for the open door that led to the Bridge.

Nilson was herding Vorshak and Preston out of the computer bay at blaster-point.

'I trusted you, Nilson,' said Vorshak angrily.

'Don't take it too hard, Commander. Doctor Solow and I were only doing our duty as we saw it – just as you are.'

The Doctor burst into the Bridge area, Tegan behind him. 'Commander, the Myrka has been destroyed –' He broke off noticing with some surprise that Nilson seemed to be covering his superior officer with a blaster. 'What's going on?'

'It seems that Nilson here is an enemy agent, Doctor,' said Vorshak bitterly.

'Enemy agent? You mean he's working for the Silurians?'

'No. For the East Bloc.'

The Doctor said impatiently. 'Look, this is no time for your petty human feuds. Do you know what you're doing, Nilson?'

'I know very well, Doctor.'

'Do you?' snapped Vorshak. 'Do you really? Before long the Sea Devils will be in control of this Base.'

'Which means they'll have control of the proton missiles,' said the Doctor.

Nilson didn't look particularly worried. 'Missiles they cannot fire. Maddox rigged the computer under my instructions. The missiles are disarmed – irreversibly.'

'Irreversibly to you, perhaps. The technology of these creatures pre-dates yours by millions of years. Believe me, if they intend to fire these missiles of yours, they'll find a means to do so!'

'They simply won't have time, Doctor. As soon as I

leave in the escape pod, this Base will be attacked by the forces of the East Bloc. Since the Base is helpless, everything in it, the creatures as well, will be destroyed.'

Suddenly Maddox appeared in the doorway to the computer bay. He was wild-eyed and hysterical, but he was sane again. For the time being at least, the savage cut-off from Nilson's device had cancelled the conditioning.

He waved the blaster at Nilson. 'You murdering traitor! You made me kill Karina. Now you're going to die.'

Nilson's hand dived into his pocket and operated the control device. Maddox swayed on his feet, desperately trying to bring the blaster to bear on Nilson.

'I'm sorry Maddox,' said Nilson softly. 'Your usefulness is at an end.' He turned the control device up to its highest frequency. Maddox's face twisted in agony, his body stiffened, and he crashed to the floor like a felled tree, his brain burned out.

Preston ran to the body. She looked up. 'He's dead.'

'Leave him,' ordered Nilson. 'Over here!'

For a moment the Doctor was forgotten. Suddenly he flung himself across the room at Nilson, knocking the blaster aside. Nilson clubbed him savagely across the head with the control device in his left hand. The Doctor staggered and fell. Before he could recover, Nilson grabbed Tegan, holding her in front of him as a shield.

'If any of you try to follow me, she dies,' he said matter-of-factly, and backed away from the Bridge.

Turlough, Bulic and a surviving guard were in full retreat by now. They dashed along the corridor, turned a corner – and then found themselves facing a squad of Sea Devils. The guard raised his weapon to fire

– and was immediately shot down.

Turlough stared for a moment in horror at the bulbous-eyed creatures and then threw down his weapon. 'Surrender, you fool,' he hissed. 'Throw down your blaster.'

Reluctantly Bulic obeyed.

The Doctor picked himself up and rubbed his aching head.

Lieutenant Preston was checking the computer.

Vorshak was listening to a report on his communicator.

'There's very little we can do, sir,' an anguished voice was saying. 'The Sea Devils have just breached the Bridge perimeter defences.'

'What about Bulic, and the boy Turlough?'

'No one's seen them, Commander. They must be dead or taken.'

Vorshak said, 'Doctor, I'm sorry . . .'

The Doctor picked up Karina's blaster from beside Maddox's body. 'I'm going after Nilson. Where's the entrance to the dock for the escape pod?'

Vorshak led him to a wall-plan of the Base. 'Here, Doctor.' His finger indicated a point on the map. 'The quickest way is along here, and then down here.'

With one quick glance the Doctor committed the map to memory and hurried on his way.

Sauvix strode proudly up to the Silurians. 'Your orders have been obeyed, Icthar. The way to the Bridge is clear.'

Turlough and Bulic had been herded into what looked like an empty store-room, with a Sea Devil guard at the door.

Turlough was by no means sure why they had been

left alive – and he had little confidence in this state of things continuing. 'We've got to get out of here, Bulic.'

Bulic, who had fought so hard and so long, seemed suddenly to have given up. He was slumped disconsolately in one corner. 'What's the point? Where could we go? The Sea Devils are all over the Base.'

Turlough was no hero, but he had the determination of a born survivor. 'We must get to the TARDIS. At least we'd be safe there, and if the Doctor can get there, we can still escape.'

There was a little window in the door. Through it Turlough could see their Sea Devil guard. He looked very alert.

Nilson was beginning to wish he'd picked a more docile hostage. His progress had been considerably slowed by the fact that Tegan had struggled every foot of the way, and she was struggling still. Nilson would cheerfully have killed her except for her possible value as a hostage. Once he reached the escape pod . . .

He shook her savagely. 'Be still, woman!'

He dragged her around the corner, and they found themselves looking at the prone body of the Myrka.

Intrigued despite his haste, Nilson paused for a second to examine the UV convertor. 'Ingenious! A pity all the Doctor's efforts were to no avail.'

'You haven't got away yet,' said Tegan spiritedly.

Nilson gripped her shoulder savagely, urging her onwards. Suddenly Tegan grabbed his arm and pulled him off balance. He lunged towards her. Tegan jumped aside, tripping him up. He fell, just as the Doctor ran around the corner.

'Tegan,' called the Doctor running forward.

'Stay where you are, Doctor,' shouted Nilson. He was still on the floor, but the blaster in his hand was levelled unerringly at Tegan. 'You were foolish to follow me, Doctor. Now drop the weapon, or the girl dies here and now.'

The Doctor tossed his blaster to the floor – he'd never liked carrying weapons anyway. 'Let Tegan go, Nilson. She's no use to you now.'

Nilson was scrambling to his feet, the blaster wavering between the Doctor and Tegan.

'Killing us won't make your escape any easier,' said the Doctor calmly. 'Fire now and you could bring every Sea Devil in the area running.'

Nilson said furiously, 'I am prepared to take that risk, Doctor.'

'Make a wish, Tegan,' said the Doctor calmly.

Nilson levelled the weapon at the Doctor's head. 'Goodbye, Doctor.'

'Goodbye,' said the Doctor.

Flinging himself to one side, he threw the switch on the UV convertor, filling the corridor with intolerable white light. Nilson screamed, covering his eyes. The Doctor jumped up, eyes half-closed against the glare.

Tegan had guessed what was going to happen and was standing there with her eyes protected by an upflung arm. The Doctor grabbed her other arm to pull her away.

Nilson fired wildly, missing by several feet, just as the Sea Devils stalked around the corner. Nilson stood staring at them, the blaster in his hand. Instantly the Sea Devils shot him down.

They advanced on the Doctor and Tegan.

10

Captured

The Doctor stepped forward to meet the advancing Sea Devils. 'How do you do? Haven't we met before? I'm the Doctor!'

There was no reply. The Doctor switched off the UV convertor and the lighting returned to normal. 'That's better. Now, take me to your leader!'

One of the Sea Devils made a gesture with the strangely shaped weapon in its hand.

The Doctor and Tegan moved back down the corridor, the Sea Devils behind them.

Turlough paced nervously up and down the bare metal room, looking round for some way of escape. He looked through the little window in the door. The Sea Devil guard was standing in the corridor with his back to them – no real chance that way.

Turlough spotted a metal grille high up in the wall. He looked down at Bulic, still slumped in his corner and pointed. 'What's that up there?'

'Must be a ventilation shaft.'

'Well, well, well,' said Turlough softly. 'Come on, up you get. I need your help.'

The Doctor and Tegan were marched back onto the Bridge. It was clear that the Base was now in the invaders' hands. Vorshak stood by the command console, flanked by two brown-skinned alien figures with crested heads – Silurians!

The Doctor looked at the blunter, more rounded heads of his Sea Devil guards, at the crest that swept backwards and downwards from the reptilian snouts.

Silurians *and* Sea Devils, thought the Doctor. He had encountered both before, but separately. Now they had resumed their old alliance. It was doubtful if the human race had ever faced more formidable enemies.

The leader of the Sea Devil guards raised his hand in salute. 'Greetings, Icthar. My Warriors have now captured the reactor room.'

The taller of the Silurians said, 'Excellent, Sauvix. You have done well.'

'All right, so you've won,' said Vorshak savagely. 'You might at least allow my crew members to surrender, rather than just hunt them down.'

'It is they who insist on fighting,' said Icthar blandly.

He sounded, thought the Doctor, as though it made little difference whether the crew of the Base surrendered or were shot down, as if it would all come to the same thing in the end.

Another Silurian emerged from the computer bay. 'The damage has been assessed, Icthar. The computer can be returned to normal functioning.'

'Excellent,' said the tall Silurian again. 'See that the work is completed with all speed, Tarpok.'

The Silurian returned to the computer bay.

'Icthar,' muttered the Doctor. 'Icthar! I recognise that name.'

Tegan looked at him in amazement. 'You *know* that – *thing?*'

'I think so. I thought he'd been killed with the

others.'

Icthar seemed to notice the Doctor and Tegan for the first time. 'Remove these prisoners from the Bridge,' he ordered.

The Doctor stepped forward. 'Wait, Icthar. We are known to each other.'

For a moment the huge Silurian eyes were turned upon the Doctor, then: 'You are mistaken,' said Icthar. 'Take him away.'

'No, wait,' shouted the Doctor. 'I am a Time Lord, Icthar, my race changes, regenerates. In an earlier incarnation you knew me as the Doctor.'

'*You* are the Doctor?' said Icthar slowly. 'You can prove what you say?'

'When we last met over a hundred years ago, I came to the underground base of your people, I tried to mediate, to make peace between you and the humans.'

The Doctor talked on, recalling the events of that crisis of long ago. He remembered the wise old leader he had known as the Old Silurian, the arrogantly hostile Young Silurian.

Icthar had been the third member of the ruling group. He had said little and the Doctor had always felt that he was poised between the two opposing factions.

'You were one of the noble Silurian Triad,' concluded the Doctor. 'I feared you had all been killed –'

The Doctor broke off, remembering that the peace negotiations had broken down, ending in disaster. Without the Doctor's knowledge or consent, the Brigadier had set off charges that entombed the Silurians in their underground base.

The Doctor looked at the Sea Devils remembering their earlier attack on the humans, encouraged by the Master. There too the Doctor's peacemaking efforts

102

had met with small success. They had been sabotaged by a treacherous attack ordered by an ambitious human politician. The Doctor and the Master had escaped from the Sea Devils' undersea base – and the Doctor had been forced to ensure that the base blew up behind them.

'So you are the Doctor,' said Icthar finally. 'You betrayed us, Doctor. You have much to answer for.'

'Twice I have tried in vain to make peace between your people and the human race,' admitted the Doctor. 'Twice I have failed, thanks to the self-destructive efforts of the extremists on both sides. Must it happen again? Please, Icthar, may we speak?'

Icthar considered for a moment. 'The Doctor and Commander Vorshak may remain. Let the others be removed.'

Tegan and Lieutenant Preston were marched out by Sea Devil guards.

'I will listen to what you have to say, Doctor,' said Icthar. 'But I should tell you that we have long abandoned the way of peace and mediation.'

'So it seems. But why? Why is a civilised race like yours waging unprovoked war?'

'Defensive war,' corrected Icthar. 'Silurian law forbids any other. There is a distinction.'

'Defensive war? There's no such thing. When we last met, your leaders were at least prepared to consider living in peace with the other inhabitants of this planet. There are vast portions of the land and of the seas that the humans will never use. At least some of your leaders agreed that there was room for both races. Why abandon such an enlightened policy now?'

'The aim of our policy has always been the peaceful survival of the Silurian race, Doctor. It still is. All that has changed is the means by which it is to be achieved.'

'By actions such as we have seen here? The unprovoked attack on this Sea Base?'

'You forget, Doctor, that twice, at your urging, we offered the hand of peace to these ape-descended primitives. Twice we were attacked and treacherously slaughtered. It will not happen again.'

'But peaceful co-existence between Man and Silurian is the only way. There is no other solution.'

'There is, Doctor. A final solution.'

The chilling words filled the Doctor with sudden horror. 'Genocide? Everything you Silurians hold sacred forbids it.'

'*We* shall not destroy the humans, Doctor. The ape-primitives will destroy themselves. We shall merely provide them with the pretext for doing so.'

Suddenly the Doctor understood everything. 'You're going to fire the proton missiles! Trigger off the war this Base was designed to fight!'

'Precisely, Doctor. And these *humans* will die as they have lived – in a sea of their own blood.'

Turlough, at least, had no intention of dying. Like a rat in a trap he would go on struggling till the very last moment.

He was standing on Bulic's shoulders, wrenching desperately at the grille that covered the air-vent. With no other tools than a small penknife, it was a long hard job, but when his own life was at stake Turlough spared no efforts.

There was a noise outside the cell and Turlough sprang to the ground. He heard a familiar voice. 'Get off me! Leave me alone!' The door was flung open. Tegan and Preston were thrust into the room by a Sea Devil. The door slammed behind them.

Tegan gave Turlough a hug. 'Turlough! You're alive!'

Turlough was in no mood for sentimental greetings. 'Alive and well and trying to escape. Will one of you keep a watch please?'

'I'll do it,' said Preston. She stationed herself at the door.

'Right,' said Turlough. 'Tegan, you help Bulic to lift me up . . .'

In an amazingly short time, Tarpok came out of the computer bay. 'The primary circuits of the computer are now functioning, Icthar.'

'Can we now activate the missile data banks?'

'We will need the Commander's hand-scan for clearance.'

Vorshak thrust his hands behind his back. 'You'll get no help from me, Silurian.'

A Sea Devil moved forward menacingly, and Icthar said, 'Your hand-scan, Commander. I will not ask again.'

'I suggest you do as he says,' said the Doctor.

'No.' Vorshak stood firm, hands behind his back, quite prepared for a heroic death.

'Listen,' said the Doctor quietly. 'Do you know how strong those things are? They'll manage to use your hand-scan, even if they have to kill you in the process. And remember, while there's life, there's hope.'

Vorshak looked at the Doctor for a long moment. Then, resignedly, he moved to the command console and put his hand into the hand-scan recess.

'Thank you, Doctor,' said Icthar.

Vorshak stepped away from the console and moved closer to the Doctor. 'You know why I gave in?' he whispered. 'Those missiles will never leave the launch pads, not without a synch operator to complete the firing sequence.'

'Don't be too sure of that.'

105

'I tell you it's impossible, Doctor. That's the way the system is designed. A synch operator is our insurance against an unauthorised missile launch.'

The Doctor indicated a complex piece of Silurian equipment connected to the computer console. 'If my guess is right, that thing is a Manipulator, a little piece of Silurian gadgetry that will more than make up for the lack of a synch operator – unless we can do something about it . . .'

Turlough gave a final heave, and the grille of the ventilation shaft came away. Passing it down to Tegan, he jumped down and said, 'Right. The thing to do now is make our way back to the TARDIS.'

'Not the TARDIS – the Bridge.'

'What is it about you humans that makes you think there's something noble about a completely futile gesture?'

Tegan was shocked. 'Turlough!'

Bulic said scornfully. 'You would prefer that we left our colleagues – and your friends – to die?'

'Look, if there was any real chance of saving them, I'd be the first to go,' said Turlough virtuously. 'But since there isn't . . .'

'We won't know if there's a chance until we've tried,' said Tegan. She looked at Bulic. 'Come on, let's go.'

Bulic made his hands into a stirrup and lifted Tegan up so that she could scramble through the gap.

For some time the Silurian called Scibus had been working at the missile console. Now he looked up. 'The missiles are re-targeted, Icthar.'

'Excellent!'

'Launching those things will trigger off a holocaust,' protested the Doctor. 'You'll destroy everybody.'

106

'Not everybody. The Silurians will survive.'

'To be masters of a dead world?'

'The world will not be dead, Doctor, only the ape-creatures who have usurped it. Safely hidden away in deep hibernation there waits the remainder of the Silurian race, the true life-force of this planet. When our rightful position is restored, *we* shall rule the Earth once more.'

Tegan and Bulic had gone from the cell, and Turlough was pacing moodily up and down.

Lieutenant Preston turned away from the door. 'Turlough . . .'

'What?'

'They'd stand a better chance if we'd gone with them.'

'A better chance of what? Dying? Don't worry, they'll manage that nicely by themselves.'

She looked at him in silence.

'All right,' said Turlough wearily. He formed his hands into a stirrup. 'Put your foot in there and I'll lift you up.'

'What about us, Icthar?' demanded the Doctor. 'Are we going to be included in your final solution?'

'We are a just race, Doctor. Despite the failure of your peacemaking attempts, we bear you no malice. Once we are finished here, you and your companions will be released.'

'And the rest of these people – the crew of the Sea Base?'

'They will stay here to die. After all, it will be an act of mercy. Soon there will be no one alive on the surface for them to return to. Commander Vorshak, you will please join me at the command console?'

Vorshak hesitated, looking in anguish at the Doctor.

'Do it, Commander,' said the Doctor gently.

Vorshak moved to the console.

Fortunately Bulic had a good knowledge of the Base ventilation system. He led Tegan through a network of air-shafts until they emerged behind a grille in the computer bay – which was empty, since Karina's body had been taken away. Bulic kicked out the grille from the inside, climbed through and helped Tegan to get down.

He moved over to the door and opened it a fraction. He could see the Doctor standing a little apart from Icthar and Vorshak at the command console. Two Sea Devil guards stood by the Bridge door.

'They're in there,' whispered Bulic, and Tegan came over to join him.

'Initiate the test firing sequence,' ordered Icthar.

Reluctantly Vorshak put his hand in the scan recess once more, and a flood of data streamed across the read-out screen.

Somehow aware of movement behind him, the Doctor glanced over his shoulders. He saw Bulic peering at him through the door to the computer room, which stood very slightly ajar.

Bulic put a finger to his lips. The Doctor nodded, and the door closed.

'Did he see you?' whispered Tegan.

Bulic nodded. 'I don't know what he's planning, but he'd better hurry – it won't be long till they discover we've escaped . . .'

The Doctor glanced at the Sea Devil guards who stood staring impassively ahead of them. He guessed that any movement towards the Bridge door would alert them immediately. But they didn't seem to be concerned with his movements inside the complex.

Moving casually from instrument bank to instrument bank, studying one set of readings and then another with pretended fascination, the Doctor worked his way round to the door of the computer bay and slipped inside, closing it softly behind him.

Once inside, he exchanged hushed and enthusiastic greetings with Tegan and Bulic. 'Well done, both of you. Nice timing! Is Turlough safe?'

'Oh yes,' said Tegan scornfully. 'Safely skulking in his prison.'

The Doctor looked up at the open grille. 'Right you are then. Lead on.'

Bulic didn't move. 'Aren't we going to get the Commander out?'

The Doctor shook his head. 'Impossible, I'm afraid. The Silurians need him in there. He'll be watched and guarded every moment.'

'At least we can try,' said Bulic obstinately.

He moved towards the door, but the Doctor put a hand on his arm to stop him. 'We'll rescue your Commander for you – but not here, not now. We'll come back for him, I promise. Trust me.'

Bulic looked hard at him for a moment then nodded.

They moved over towards the air-vent.

'Where are we going?' asked Tegan. 'Back to the TARDIS?'

'No, to the chemical store.'

'You've got a plan, Doctor?'

'I'm afraid so. I only hope I won't have to use it.'

11

Counterattack

Turlough and Preston emerged from the ventilation system into one of the Sea Base's innumerable corridors. It was empty – except for the sprawled bodies of a couple of Sea Base guards.

Preston looked around, getting her bearings. 'This way.' She picked up one of the dead guards' blasters.

Snatching up the other guards' blaster, Turlough followed her.

Sauvix strode angrily onto the Bridge. 'The prison room is empty, Icthar. The primitives have escaped.'

'How is this possible, Sauvix? Explain.'

Sauvix was looking around the Bridge. 'Where is the Doctor?'

The Doctor was nowhere to be seen.

Icthar turned threateningly on Vorshak. 'Commander? Where is he?'

'I've no idea.'

Icthar moved over to the computer bay and opened the door. Sauvix followed him. They looked around the room, and registered the gaping entrance to the ventilation shaft.

'Find them, Sauvix,' hissed Icthar furiously. 'Find the Doctor, find the escaped primitives and kill them!'

As they hurried along the corridor, Turlough and Lieutenant Preston heard the crackle of blaster-fire.

'They must be mopping up survivors,' muttered Turlough.

'Those survivors could be your friends. Shouldn't we try to help them?'

They moved towards the sound of fire.

Not far away, the Doctor, Tegan and Bulic were also emerging from the ventilation system into a corridor.

The Doctor was the last to climb down and Tegan reached up to help him. 'Hurry, Doctor!'

Suddenly there was a whining sound. A nearby lift door slid open and two Sea Devils emerged. Raising their weapons they stalked towards the helpless Doctor and his companion.

Then Turlough and Lieutenant Preston appeared around the far corner, *behind* the Sea Devils. They raised their weapons and took aim. 'Remember,' whispered Turlough, 'Aim for the head. We won't get a second chance.'

Taking careful aim both fired almost simultaneously and both Sea Devils fell.

Once again there was a hurried exchange of greetings.

Tegan looked suspiciously at Turlough. 'What are you doing here?'

'You didn't really think I'd leave you to go it alone, did you?'

Tegan was far from convinced. But Turlough's presence pointed to some kind of change of heart. She decided to give him the benefit of the doubt. 'It never crossed my mind!'

'Where are you making for, Doctor?' asked Lieutenant Preston.

'The chemical store.'

'This way,' said Bulic, and the combined party set off.

Vorshak watched his Silurian captors intently, still hoping to find some way to frustrate their plans.

At the very least, he could make a last desperate attempt to wreck the command console. It probably wouldn't succeed, but he'd be doing *something* . . .

The complex piece of Silurian equipment was linked to the computer now, gently throbbing with energy.

'Is the computer fully operational?' asked Icthar.

The Silurian called Tarpok said. 'It is restored and tested.'

'Excellent. Then align the Manipulator to the computer.'

Tarpok began working busily at the console.

Vorshak poised himself to attack. There was very little time left.

Moving swiftly down the corridors, hiding from occasional Sea Devil patrols, the Doctor and his companions reached the chemical stores at last.

The Doctor looked round the room. 'Watch the door, Turlough.' He began examining the labels on the stacked chemical cylinders piled high all around them.

'What are you looking for?' asked Tegan.

The Doctor tapped one of the cylinders. 'This stuff here is Hexachromite — it's a deadly poison to reptiles.'

'Then isn't that what you want?'

'I want an alternative, if I can find one. Something less lethal that will do the job just as well.'

As the Doctor continued his search, Bulic asked. 'Do you know what the Silurians are planning,

Doctor?'

'Oh yes, they were very forthcoming, all in all. They intend to launch your proton missiles and trigger off the war to end all wars. A war between you humans, that is. When it's all over, the Silurians will emerge to rule the Earth.'

'Look out, Doctor!' called Turlough. 'Sea Devils!'

'Take cover, everyone,' called the Doctor softly. 'Get behind those drums.'

Seconds later a Sea Devil strode into what appeared to be an empty store room.

It stood for a moment gazing suspiciously around.

The Doctor pressed himself lower into his hiding place. Unfortunately he was hiding behind an empty drum and it shifted, very slightly.

The Sea Devil sprang forward, sweeping the drum away, to reveal the Doctor. Raising its weapon the Sea Devil fired. The Doctor flung himself aside and the blast burnt a hole in a nearby cylinder. A cloud of chemical vapour shot out enveloping the Sea Devil.

The effect was extraordinary. Dropping its weapon, the Sea Devil staggered back, clutching at the gills in its neck. Seconds later it lay dead on the floor.

The Doctor stood looking down at the body.

Tegan emerged from hiding. 'What happened?'

'Hexachromite. It does that to all forms of reptile life.'

'Then surely it's just what you want,' said Lieutenant Preston. 'Use it on the invaders.'

'And kill them all off?'

'Why not? They're about to start a war that will destroy everyone on Earth.'

'With the weapons you humans invented to destroy each other,' pointed out the Doctor. 'Sometimes I wonder why I like the people of this miserable planet so much. Don't you realise the Silurians and the Sea

Devils are ancient and noble races, with skills you pathetic humans can only dream about?'

Lieutenant Preston stared at him, astonished by the sudden outburst.

Tegan understood. The Doctor hated violence and killing. And now he was probably going to have to resort to both to save his friends.

Turlough had no doubts at all. 'What you say about the Silurians may be true, Doctor. But that doesn't make what they're going to do any more justified.'

'I know,' said the Doctor quietly. 'And I know I've got to stop them. But not with mass murder. Not if there's some other way.'

Tegan said helplessly. 'What's the alternative?'

'Something that will disable rather than kill – if only I can find it in time.'

The Doctor resumed his search.

Tarpok and Scibus were busy at the computer and command consoles.

'The Manipulator is now aligned with the computer,' said Tarpok.

'Alignment confirmed,' reported Scibus.

'Excellent,' said Icthar. 'Let us proceed.'

There was the wail of an alarm. On the main monitor screen the read-out was flashing: 'MISSILE ALERT. MISSILE ALERT.'

Icthar turned to Vorshak. 'What is happening?'

'Impossible to say. The computer has ordered a missile run. Could be a practice, could be the real thing.'

'Check the Manipulator,' ordered Icthar.

Tarpok studied the readings on the Silurian device. 'Our readings confirm that this is a computer-controlled practice missile run.'

'The time for such games is over,' said Icthar

114

scornfully. 'Activate the Manipulator and launch the missiles.'

The Doctor was still searching amongst the drums and cylinders of chemicals when the sinister sound of the alarm rang through the chemical store. 'What's that? What does it mean?'

Bulic said, 'It's a missile alert, Doctor. It means countdown is imminent.'

Turlough said, 'Well, Doctor? What are you going to do?'

The Doctor didn't reply.

'You must decide quickly, Doctor,' said Tegan. 'Billions of people could die . . .'

The Doctor sighed, accepting the inevitable. 'Yes all right. Turlough, get the grille open. Preston get one of those pumps fitted up. We'll have to feed the gas into the ventilation system.'

With frantic speed they set to work.

'The missiles are armed and targeted,' reported Scibus.

Vorshak stared at the three Silurians, unable to believe that they were really going to carry out their terrible plan. 'You're mad, all of you.'

'It is you ape-primitives who are mad,' said Icthar. '*You* have developed this weaponry. We cannot be held responsible for it.'

'Contact the heads of governments,' urged Vorshak. 'Make your demands, tell them you want a share of the Earth. They'll listen.'

'Your race has had its chance,' said Icthar implacably.

'Please, try one more time, for pity's sake.'

'It is too late for pity,' said Icthar. 'It is much too late.'

In the chemical store the pump was humming steadily, feeding Hexachromite gas into the ventilation system.

The Doctor said thoughtfully, 'Of course, it will take some time for the gas to spread.'

'Will it work fast enough?' asked Tegan anxiously. 'How long before it floods the whole Base?'

'I rather hope that won't be necessary. If I can get back to the Bridge, I may still be able to reason with Icthar, persuade him to abandon the missile launch.'

Turlough looked at him in amazement. 'You're mad, Doctor. You've tried that once already, remember?'

'Ah, but this time I'll have a counter-threat to back up my arguments,' said the Doctor, hopeful as ever.

Icthar studied the flow of data across the screen. He looked almost pityingly at Vorshak. 'Soon it will be all over.'

Vorshak stared at him in silent anguish, poised to make a last-minute attack.

Suddenly Tarpok called, 'There is computer resistance to the Manipulator.'

Hope flared up in Vorshak. 'I told you you'd never succeed!'

'Increase the power, Tarpok,' said Icthar placidly. 'It seems that your computers are as stubborn as you humans, Commander. But do not be deceived. We shall overcome you both in the end.'

The Doctor stood watching sadly as the pump drove the deadly gas into the ventilation system. 'Right, that's it, I want the rest of you to go back to the TARDIS and wait for me. You left the door ajar, Lieutenant Preston?'

She nodded.

The Doctor went on, 'You'll be safe inside the TARDIS whatever happens.'

The siren rang out again, this time with a different note.

'They've changed to yellow alert,' said Bulic.

The Doctor nodded. 'We must go.' He looked round the little group. 'Good luck, all of you. I'll join you in the TARDIS as soon as I can. If I don't – Tegan and Turlough will have to do the best they can.'

They heard a voice behind them. 'So Doctor, I have found you!'

They turned.

Sauvix, leader of the Sea Devils was standing in the doorway.

12

Sacrifice

On the Bridge all eyes were fixed on the read-out screen, on the flashing words 'YELLOW ALERT'. Incongruously the Intercom beeped.

Icthar touched a control. 'Speak!'

They heard Sauvix's voice. 'I have the Doctor, Icthar.'

'And you have your orders,' said Icthar implacably. Kill him.' He turned back to the screen.

'Sauvix, you must listen to me,' pleaded the Doctor.

There was a gleam of what might have been amusement in the great bulbous eyes. 'No, Doctor. *You* must die. But first, switch off that pump.'

As the Doctor moved towards the pump, Lieutenant Preston looked swiftly around her.

Turlough had laid his blaster-rifle on top of one of the cylinders. It wasn't all that far from her . . .

As Sauvix's weapon moved to cover the Doctor, she made a desperate lunge for the blaster. She snatched it up, aimed . . .

Sauvix whirled round and shot her down.

As Preston died, her hand tightened on the trigger of the blaster. It fired, burning a hole in a cylinder close to Sauvix's head.

The gas spurted out. Sauvix reeled, clutching his gills, and fell dying to the floor.

Tegan was kneeling by Lieutenant Preston's body. 'She's dead, Doctor.'

The Doctor nodded sadly. 'Such a waste.'

'She saved your life,' said Tegan. 'Don't let her sacrifice it for nothing.'

'I won't. I must get to the Bridge!'

'You'll need some help. We'll come with you, won't we Turlough?'

Turlough nodded resignedly. As far as he could see, anywhere on the Base was just about as dangerous as anywhere else.

'All right,' said the Doctor. 'Bring some of those oxygen packs. We may need them.' He pointed to a wall-rack which held oxygen cylinders with attached face-masks – presumably some kind of rescue kit.

Turlough and Tegan took an oxygen pack each.

Bulic said, 'I'll stay here and keep things running. Good luck, Doctor.'

They hurried away.

The computer has stabilised,' said Scibus.

Tarpok said, 'Confirmed. The Manipulator has regained control.'

'You see, Commander?' said Icthar triumphantly. 'Now do you believe me? Silurian technology is invincible.'

Despairingly, Vorshak turned away.

The Doctor, Tegan and Turlough turned a corner just in time to see two Sea Devil guards stagger helplessly and collapse. Just above their heads, a cloud of gas drifted mistily from the ventilation grille.

'It's working!' said Turlough.

The Doctor frowned. 'It's working far too quickly. I

can't bargain with Icthar if all his guards are dead.'

If all his guards are dead, we won't need to bargain, thought Turlough. Keeping the thought to himself, he followed Tegan and the Doctor down the corridor.

The countdown to missile launch had reached its final phase. All that was needed now was the final hand-print of the base Commander.

'Fetch him,' ordered Icthar.

Two Sea Devil guards seized Vorshak and dragged him towards the command console.

'No!' shouted Vorshak. 'No! I will not be responsible for the destruction of my own kind.'

But there was nothing he could do. For all his size and strength, Vorshak was like a child in the hands of the Sea Devils. They forced his hand into the hand-scan recess.

'The final phase,' said Icthar softly. 'It is almost done.'

Bulic checked the gauge on the gas cylinder. It was almost empty. Swiftly he uncoupled the cylinder, rolled it away, heaved a full one into place and connected it up.

Bulic had little faith in the Doctor's peacemaking efforts, and little interest in their success. As far as he was concerned the Hexachromite gas would deal with the Silurians very nicely.

The words 'RED ALERT' flashed on the screen.

Icthar moved slowly over to the command console. He reached out for the lever that would initiate the missile launch. Like his fellow Silurians, he was too absorbed to notice the gas-mist seeping from the ventilation grilles above his head.

He paused, savouring the moment – and the Doctor

and his companion dashed onto the Bridge.

Icthar was about to order the guards to fire, when quite suddenly he changed his mind. 'Disarm them,' he ordered.

A Sea Devil snatched the blaster from Turlough's hand.

'Welcome, Doctor,' said Icthar. 'You are just in time to witness the missile launch.'

'Wait,' said the Doctor. 'You have been defeated, Icthar. Your warriors are dying all over this Base. Abandon the Base and save yourselves.'

Icthar stared unbelievingly at him. 'The Silurians defeated? Are you mad?'

Tegan pointed to the cloud of gas drifting from the ventilation grille. 'Look at that – it's Hexachromite gas.'

'Abandon the launch,' urged the Doctor. 'Leave the Base now, while there's still time to save your own lives.'

'It is unimportant that we die,' said Icthar hoarsely. 'There are millions more in hibernation, ready to replace us.'

'And who will replace *you*, Icthar? With you dies the last of the Triad, custodians of the ideals of your race. What will become of your people then?'

'You talk in vain, Doctor,' roared Icthar. He turned to his guards. 'Kill them. Kill them now!'

The Sea Devils raised their weapons, but their movements were slow and clumsy. They staggered helplessly for a moment, and then one by one they fell.

The Doctor moved to the intercom and flicked the switch. 'Bulic, can you hear me? This is the Doctor. It's over, Bulic. Turn off the gas.'

Icthar stared wildly at him, scarcely realising what was happening. He caught a whiff of the drifting gas, staggered and then recovered himself. 'Scibus! Begin ignition,' he ordered.

Scibus too was affected by the gas. With a last desperate effort he threw the lever. 'Missiles set,' gasped Scibus, and then crashed to the ground.

Icthar staggered and fell.

The Doctor ran to the Manipulator which was pulsing steadily. Tarpok lunged at him, but the movement was slow and clumsy. The Doctor dodged round him with ease, and Tarpok too collapsed.

The Doctor bent over the console. 'The missiles are set to fire, Vorshak. How long have we got?'

Vorshak looked at the digital countdown clock. It stood in 179. 'Less than three minutes.'

'What's the abort procedure?'

'A phased electrical charge aimed directly at the ignition circuit. It restores the launch to a simulation.'

'Then do it – right away!'

'Impossible, Doctor. Only a trained synch operator can do it, and Maddox is dead.'

The Doctor was already heading for the synch-op chair. 'All right then, I'll have to do it myself.'

'Doctor, you can't. The computer will burn out your brain in seconds.'

'Do you have a better idea?'

'All right, Doctor,' said Vorshak. 'Get into the chair.'

The Doctor settled himself in the synch-op chair, and lowered the helmet over his head. He could feel the metal terminals inside the helmet pressing into his skull. If only the link-up was close enough . . .

Tegan looked on appalled. 'Can't you disconnect the computer, Doctor?'

'I'm afraid not, Tegan, there just isn't time.'

Vorshak said, 'He's right. We're already on final countdown to ignition.'

The clock stood at 139, 138, 137 . . .

Even at the moment of greatest danger, the Doctor had time to think about the fate of his enemies. 'Tegan, Turlough. Look after the Silurians. Try giving them oxygen.'

Tegan and Turlough exchanged glances. It seemed ridiculous to worry about saving Silurian lives at this date, but it didn't seem the time to argue. Obediently they knelt beside Tarpok and Scibus and began trying to revive them with the oxygen packs.

Vorshak was busy at the computer console. 'I can perform the manual tasks, Doctor, but you'll have to do the rest. Are you ready?'

The Doctor nodded.

The clock read 119, 118, 117 . . .

'Good luck, Doctor!' Vorshak pressed the switch.

The headpiece began to glow and crackle with energy. The Doctor's body went rigid and his face twisted as the massive data input assaulted his brain.

'The strain's too great,' said Turlough. 'He'll never manage it.'

Vorshak was studying his read-out screen. 'It's working! His mind is synchronised with the computer. Doctor, can you hear me?'

The Doctor nodded, his face set with strain.

Vorshak glanced at the clock: 100, 99, 98 . . .

'I'm going to switch you through to the ignition circuit.' His hands moved over the controls. 'Right, I've isolated the ignition circuit, Doctor. See if you can identify it. Nod if you can.'

The Doctor nodded.

'Now, concentrate, Doctor,' urged Vorshak. 'I'm going to feed in the charge. You must concentrate and direct it, to burn out the circuit.'

The Doctor nodded again.

The clock ticked on: 60, 59, 58 . . .

Icthar was close to death, but he could not, would

not die with his task unfinished. Moving with agonising slowness, he reached out for a weapon that had fallen from the hands of one of the dead Sea Devils. Slowly, agonisingly, Icthar crawled towards it . . .

Abandoning all hope of reviving her Silurian, Tegan looked up – and saw Icthar swaying to his feet, weapon in hand. 'Turlough,' she screamed.

Shakily Icthar aimed the weapon at the Doctor. Then Vorshak stepped forward, shielding him. Turlough was already on the move. He sprang forwards and grabbed the blaster, just as Icthar fired . . .

Vorshak staggered for a moment, then steadied himself, gripping the edge of the console.

Turlough snatched the blaster from the weakened Icthar and shot him down at point-blank range.

Vorshak's voice sounded unnaturally calm. 'Listen to me carefully, Doctor. The charge *must* be in phase with the pulse of the circuit. If not, it will destroy you. Concentrate, Doctor. Let nothing distract you.'

He shot a glance at the clock: 30, 29, 28 . . .

Vorshak threw another switch and a surge of energy crackled through the terminals of the Doctor's helmet. His body shook, his face twisted with concentration.

10, 9, 8, 7, 6 . . .

'Now Doctor,' shouted Vorshak. 'Now!'

5, 4, 3, 2, 1 . . . The read-out screen went blank.

Suddenly the words 'ABORT. ABORT. ABORT. LAUNCH CANCELLED' were flashing from the screen. The headpiece rose up automatically and the Doctor slumped back in his chair.

'You've done it,' said Vorshak softly. Slowly, painfully he moved closer to the screen. 'Mission cancelled.' He looked wonderingly round at the others. 'He did it,' said Commander Vorshak, and slumped forwards over the dead body of Icthar.

Tegan was shaking the Doctor's shoulder. 'Doctor, are you all right?'

The Doctor opened his eyes and smiled at her.

'Turlough, he's alive!' said Tegan joyfully.

Turlough was examining Vorshak. 'The Commander wasn't so lucky. He must have been hit when Icthar fired.'

The Doctor got shakily to his feet. 'Did I succeed?' he asked dazedly.

Tegan ran to his side. 'Yes, Doctor. Look!' She pointed to the screen with its 'MISSION CANCELLED' message.

The Doctor nodded, but there was no triumph, no pleasure in his face.

Turlough was staring around the room, taking in the full extent of the tragedy. 'They're all dead, you know,' he said wonderingly.

So many dead, thought the Doctor sadly: the traitors Nilson and Solow; Maddox, their helpless pawn, and his victim, Karina; Lieutenant Preston; all the crew members killed in the attack; and now Commander Vorshak himself. Then there were those other deaths that would always be on the Doctor's conscience: the Sea Devil guards, and Sauvix, their leader; the Silurians Tarpok and Scibus; Icthar, their leader, last of the great Silurian Triad.

Bulic at least had survived and there would be other human survivors, scattered about the Base. Bulic would have to take charge, explain what had happened to the astonished rescuers from the surface.

Still, at least the missiles had not been launched.

Mankind had not destroyed itself – not this time. They would go back to the TARDIS, decided the Doctor, repair it, leave without fuss and look for some happier place, some more peaceful time. He took a last look at the bodies of Vorshak and Icthar.

'There should have been another way,' said the Doctor sadly. He led the way from the Bridge.

DOCTOR WHO

	TERRANCE DICKS	
0426114558	**Doctor Who and The Abominable Snowmen**	£1.35
0426200373	**Doctor Who and The Android Invasion**	£1.25
0426201086	**Doctor Who and The Androids of Tara**	£1.35
	IAN MARTER	
0426116313	**Doctor Who and The Ark In Space**	£1.35
	TERRANCE DICKS	
0426201043	**Doctor Who and The Armageddon Factor**	£1.35
0426112954	**Doctor Who and The Auton Invasion**	£1.50
0426116747	**Doctor Who and The Brain of Morbius**	£1.35
0426110250	**Doctor Who and The Carnival of Monsters**	£1.35
	MALCOLM HULKE	
042611471X	**Doctor Who and The Cave Monsters**	£1.50
	TERRANCE DICKS	
0426117034	**Doctor Who and The Claws of Axos**	£1.35
	DAVID FISHER	
042620123X	**Doctor Who and The Creature from the Pit**	£1.35
	DAVID WHITAKER	
0426113160	**Doctor Who and The Crusaders**	£1.50
	BRIAN HAYLES	
0426200616	**Doctor Who and The Curse of Peladon**	£1.50
	GERRY DAVIS	
0426114639	**Doctor Who and The Cybermen**	£1.50
	BARRY LETTS	
0426113322	**Doctor Who and The Daemons**	£1.50

Prices are subject to alteration

STAR Books are obtainable from many booksellers and newsagents. If you have any difficulty please send purchase price plus postage on the scale below to:-

>Star Cash Sales
>P.O. Box 11
>Falmouth
>Cornwall
>OR
>Star Book Service,
>G.P.O. Box 29,
>Douglas,
>Isle of Man,
>British Isles.

While every effort is made to keep prices low, it is sometimes necessary to increase prices at short notice. Star Books reserve the right to show new retail prices on covers which may differ from those advertised in the text or elsewhere.

Postage and Packing Rate
UK: 45p for the first book, 20p for the second book and 14p for each additional book ordered to a maximum charge of £1.63. BFPO and EIRE: 45p for the first book, 20p for the second book, 14p per copy for the next 7 books thereafter 8p per book. Overseas: 75p for the first book and 21p per copy for each additional book.